ENFORCER

When ex-Vietnam veteran Washington T. Diamond quits working as racketeer Leon Greco's 'enforcer', he and his nightclub singer girlfriend Chelsea are drawn into a web of danger. Greco exerts a vicious reprisal, but Diamond receives support from Cave, a police detective, who sets him up as a private investigator. But Cave is only using Diamond as a pawn to bring down Greco's empire. Diamond becomes the bait when Greco takes out a contract on him, and he needs all his jungle experience to stay alive . . .

Books by Sydney J. Bounds
in the Linford Mystery Library:

TERROR RIDES THE WEST WIND
TWO TIMES MURDER

SYDNEY J. BOUNDS

ENFORCER

Complete and Unabridged

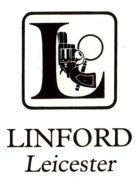

LINFORD
Leicester

First published in Great Britain

First Linford Edition
published 2006

British Library CIP Data

Bounds, Sydney J.
  Enforcer.—Large print ed.—
  Linford mystery library
  1. Detective and mystery stories
  2. Large type books
  I. Title
  823.9′14 [F]

  ISBN 1–84617–148–2

Published by
F. A. Thorpe (Publishing)
Anstey, Leicestershire

Set by Words & Graphics Ltd.
Anstey, Leicestershire
Printed and bound in Great Britain by
T. J. International Ltd., Padstow, Cornwall

This book is printed on acid-free paper

1

Bone-Breaker

The trumpet cut through a fog of tobacco smoke like a knife through flesh.

Washington T. Diamond leaned forward on a hard wooden chair placed behind and to one side of the Joe Baker Rhythm Quintet on a raised platform at the back of the long room.

A quick four-bar beat set his feet tapping. Joe was in great form, and the way he hit the top notes made Diamond's thick black fingers dance on the valves of the trumpet cradled in his lap. His eyes shone with anticipation as he waited for the bandleader to cue him to come in. So it was amateur night . . . it was still no small honour to be invited to sit in at a session with professional jazzmen.

The *Black Swan*, off Bourbon Street, rocked to an integrated blast of sound; the animal growl of muted trombone, the

1

blare of Joe's horn, shrilling clarinet, a solid rhythmic beat from the drummer and a twanging banjo. The individual sounds merged to make the club's barn of a hall throb like a cat on a hot tin roof as the band belted out Dixieland jazz.

Candlelight gleamed on brass instruments. A waiter holding a tray of drinks above his head pushed between close-set tables to reach the dais. Fans clapped and stamped their approval.

The air was humid; a sheen of sweat glistened on Diamond's chocolate-dark face and his brightly-coloured Hawaiian shirt stuck to his skin. He was only half-aware of the crowded tables, swaying bodies and tapping feet as he pursed his lips ready for the mouthpiece as Chelsea stepped up and grasped the microphone stand in both hands.

Brown-skinned Chelsea Hull was small and busty and glowed in a dazzling orange gown. Her shoes beat a tattoo and her hips swivelled on roller-bearings as she unhooked the mike and cradled it close to her lips. Her smile was like an arc-light suddenly switched on.

The quintet finished improvising and swigged beer and took puffs on half-concealed cigarettes, then swung into the opening bars of Chelsea's number. Joe Baker wheeled around and flourished his horn at Diamond.

Washington T. Diamond came up from his seat as though on springs, trumpet lifting, tall and solid as a grizzly bear. His broad face split in a grin, flashing white teeth, and he blew a slow sad accompaniment to Chelsea's throaty singing:

'I'm just a gal without a home,
Just a poor gal got no home,
Got no lover to take me home,
A poor sad gal 'vermore to roam.'

Diamond took a solo after the verse, feeling relaxed and on top of the world. Using a mute, he produced a sound full of sorrow, a lost soul moaning in the night. Then a waiter tapped his arm and whispered, 'Phone, Wash.'

Diamond frowned at the interruption and carried his horn with him as he edged between tables to the bar and picked up the telephone.

'Yeah?'

The voice at the other end of the line was carefully neutral, a grey voice owned by a grey man.

Diamond listened to instructions, said, 'Yeah . . . okay . . . '

Replacing the receiver, he moved back through the tables to the bandstand and handed Chelsea his horn.

'Got to work, baby.' Her lips made a moue of disapproval. 'Greco?'

'Yeah.'

'See you later, Wash?'

Diamond nodded as he slipped on a lightweight jacket. 'My place, okay?' He straightened his gaudy tie and left the club.

Outside, the air smelt of pizza, hamburger and spicy Cajun food, and the dark of evening fluoresced with red, green and blue neon. Bourbon Street seethed with tourists looking for a good time.

All thought of jazz faded from Diamond's mind and his face became serious as he turned into a narrow street leading down towards the river.

He hadn't used his car for the date at the *Black Swan* and loped with a pantherish grace through the underbelly of New Orleans' French Quarter, past porno and sex shops and strip shows. The whole section was a plastic and concrete jungle, different from Vietnam, but just as dangerous for the unwary.

The clinging humid heat meant that windows remained open, an invitation to thieves, and a drifting sea mist offered cover for their activities. Street lamps were sparse and shadows gathered between them. Pushers and hustlers and pimps, white, brown and black-skinned, lingered in doorways. No one bothered him as he passed, silent and wary; his size discouraged muggers.

A police car was parked at an intersection and, beyond a row of old buildings with dark shutters and wrought-iron balconies, a neon sign flashed its message:

NICK'S ARCADE
Open Twenty Four Hours Every Day

5

Even before he reached the wide open doors, he could hear a ceaseless mechanical clatter of slot machines.

The interior was crowded; row after row of silver machines were played by middle-aged women, teenagers in stone-washed jeans and school children, feeding coins in a steady flow and pulling handles with reflexes as mechanical as the machines they seemed part of. Their expressions grim, oblivious of the real world outside, they might have been robots. A player hit the jackpot and a stream of quarters tinkled when the machine paid off — to be fed straight in again. Diamond's nose wrinkled in distaste as he passed an older woman standing in a puddle; with blue-rinsed hair and rings sparkling on her fingers, she appeared unaware of her incontinence.

He carved a path through the crowded aisle to an office at the rear.

Nick sat behind a broad desk, his paunch pushing a soft chair back against the wall. His black and gleaming hair contrasted with an unhealthy pallor of skin; a sweat-stained shirt was open at the neck, his tie loosened. He gave a brief nervous smile of recognition as Diamond approached.

There were two other men in the boxlike office. The money-changer, grey-haired, with a worn leather satchel slung by a strap in front of him; and a youth wearing a brown leather jacket studded with metal stars.

Diamond automatically noted the position of each and then ignored them. He towered over the manager of the arcade.

'Mr. Greco sends a message — '

Nick interrupted hurriedly. 'Listen, I can explain. It's just a simple misunder-standing — '

Diamond's focus of attention shifted as, through the racket of the slot machines, he heard the faint click of a switch knife. The youth began to pick his teeth with the four-inch blade, his expression bored and his macho stance picked up from street films.

'Put it away, kid, or I'll ram it down your throat.'

'Says who?'

Diamond stared him down, baring his teeth. The youth regarded the large and menacing size of him and retracted the blade into its handle. His sneer froze. Diamond gave his attention back to Nick.

'Mr. Greco sends a reminder to keep your fingers out of his till. He doesn't like managers who take their cut before handing over the cash.'

Nick spread his hands, palms up, in supplication. 'If you'll just listen — '

Diamond kicked the office door shut. 'We don't want to disturb the customers, do we?'

He reached for Nick's nearest arm with big hands, lifted it and bent it backwards. The arcade manager's face turned abruptly pale and he came out of his chair, following his arm.

'No, don't . . . please!'

Diamond placed the arm across his knee and continued to bend it against the elbow joint, effortlessly. Nick pored sweat and gave a scream that was lost in the clatter of slot machines. His arm snapped like brittle toffee and he slumped in a dead faint. Diamond let him fall as though he were an empty sack.

He glanced casually at the old money-changer and the youth, who had suddenly lost his macho toughness.

'When Nick comes round, tell him Mr. Greco said to stay in line.'

He opened the door and walked from the office, bulled his way through the crowded aisle and out to the street.

★ ★ ★

Chelsea Hull left the jazz club carrying Diamond's trumpet in its case, climbed into her white Datsun and drove away. The night was hot and airless, but the mist had cleared and the sky was sprinkled with stars.

She turned down a narrow street where apartment dwellers sprawled on sidewalks, and felt for them. She could remember a time, before she got regular well-paid work as a singer, when she too could not afford air-conditioning.

And before that as a country girl, the poverty, growing out of her only dress and holes in her shoes, the rats and

9

continual hunger — days when a half-loaf of stale bread was a feast.

When she was young she'd always enjoyed joining in the gospel singing at the black church, and that had started her off. Then she'd heard records of Jessie Smith and Billie Holiday and those blues singers revved her up till her blood ran hot and she knew what she wanted to do with her life.

She was fourteen when she left home and hitched a lift to New Orleans. Her first job had been with a third-rate band that gave her experience and barely enough to survive on till she moved to a nightclub. And that had been a stepping-stone to the *Black Swan*, where she'd met Wash and they'd hit it off right from the start.

Chelsea reached North Rampart Street and the statue of Satchmo at the entrance to Armstrong Park, and swung into a tiny square where a shiny new condominium towered above the older buildings.

She drove down a winding concrete slope to an underground garage, parked, and took the elevator up to Diamond's apartment. She let herself in with her own key, shivered in the icy blast of air-conditioning. It was an expensive bachelor pad, but he got paid a lot of money as Leon Greco's enforcer.

Chelsea gave a small troubled frown. Greco was one mean man from what she'd heard and she felt glad he didn't have a stake in the *Black Swan*. But, at least he paid real money.

She switched on the lights, placed Wash's trumpet case on a low table and went to the window. She stood a moment looking out across the city at the glittering grid of a thousand lighted windows and the dark crescent of the Mississippi, then drew heavy drapes.

Everything in the apartment was neat and tidy, books stacked on shelves, records in their sleeves. The carpeting was wall-to wall and luxuriously thick, furniture sparse but high quality. She put Ella's version of *Stompin' at the Savoy* on the turntable and hummed along with it.

She looked in the bedroom and the wide double bed was as tightly made as any in a hospital ward. The tiled bathroom with sunken tub was spotless.

Chelsea was inclined to be offhand about her own housekeeping, but her man seemed ready to take off at five minutes notice. She guessed that was what the army did for you. But he was a good lover and, if she disapproved of his job, she kept her mind off what he might be doing.

He was big enough — and strong enough — to take care of himself.

When she went through to the all-electric kitchen with its stainless steel fittings and outsize deep freeze, a short-haired ginger cat rubbed against her leg and miaowed plaintively. Two kittens peeked warily from beneath the stove. She sniffed at the smell from the kitty-litter tray; Chelsea didn't much like cats but she knew Wash did. The ginger cat began to claw demandingly.

'Get away, damn you.'

The door opened and Diamond walked in. 'Love me, love my cats, baby.'

He opened the fridge, used a can-opener and tipped cat-food into a dish.

The Ella Fitzgerald record ended and

the machine switched itself off. Chelsea ran water into the bathtub went into the bedroom and turned back the top cover. She slipped off her orange gown and sat on the edge of the bed in a white bra and bikini pants.

Diamond leaned against the door-frame, smiling his approval of her shapely coffee-coloured legs.

She reached behind to unfasten her bra, and paused.

'If all you're going to do is stare,' she said tartly, 'I might as well go home.'

2

Kid Stuff

Even though the old Plymouth was parked in shade, and the front windows were wound all the way down, the interior still felt like an oven. Detective Fred Cave sat behind the wheel, one arm resting on a window frame, looking out across the levee to the docks along from Canal Street.

He had a cheeseburger in one hand, a can of Heineken in the other and indigestion. Since his wife had left him, he seemed to exist solely on fast food; but at least he was out of the office. Anything was better than sitting at a desk typing up reports in triplicate. He wondered what he would do when he retired — if he retired — a job in security? Set himself up as a private investigator? That might bear thinking about.

Cave was short and thin with a face as

14

wrinkled as and the colour of a walnut. His suit needed pressing and a battered Panama was pushed back to reveal receding hair. His expression looked as sour as his stomach felt.

From time to time he let his gaze drift across the area, but it was not the wharves and cranes nor the cargo ships that interested him. He was parked across from an old warehouse, now converted for use as a factory churning out video pornography.

Roach was the name of the nominal owner, but Cave knew he was only a front for Leon Greco. It would be nice to pick up Greco some day, but Cave had no illusions; a smooth-talking lawyer would spring him faster than the speed of sound. Greco, a man with his fingers in a lot of pies, kept a safe distance from anything that might implicate him. A careful man who worked hard at earning his nickname: 'The Fox'.

The Plymouth's door opened quietly and a skinny man wearing denims and an offwhite shirt slid into the back.

'D'you have to park where you're so

easy to spot?' he complained. 'I don't want everybody to know we're doing business.'

Cave didn't bother to answer. He watched his informer in the rearview mirror. 'Breeze' wore his sandy hair long and floppy to hide a lop-sided face. At one time, Greco's hard men had worked him over and Breeze, vicious as only a small-time crook can be, sought any way to hit back, even to informing the police.

'The Fox ain't so clever any more,' Breeze said in a voice that revealed considerable satisfaction. 'More than one of his managers is ripping him off.'

Cave slung the rest of his burger away, drained his beer and set the can on the floor between his feet. He fished a packet of Marlboro's from his jacket pocket, lit two cigarettes and passed one back.

'So?'

Breeze took a long drag and feathered smoke. 'So he has to clamp down real hard, and soon, or — ' The informer made a chopping motion with one hand.

'I heard about Nick.'

'Yeah, Wash took him.'

16

Cave gave some thought to Greco's negro enforcer and wondered if there was any way of getting at him.

'Is that all you've got for me?'

'Jeez, what more d'you want? Now's the time to pull out all stops and hit the Fox good.'

'Maybe.'

Breeze slid from the back of the car and vanished into the crowd swarming towards the ferry. Cave admired the way he pulled his invisible man stunt, began to cough and stubbed out his cigarette. He brooded on what he'd just heard.

★   ★   ★

Diamond came from the bathroom and looked down at Chelsea, still asleep in bed. The drapes were drawn back and sunlight streamed into the room, giving smooth brown shoulders a golden glow. Her Afro-styled hair and eyes were covered by a pillow and, curled up, she looked petite and defenceless and aroused his protective instinct. He had a gut feeling that this girl was going to mean

17

more to him than a casual sleeping partner.

The telephone rang and he grabbed it on the second ring, before it could wake her, and glanced at the wall clock. He was late this morning.

The carefully neutral voice of Leon Greco said: 'Pierre's, the restaurant on Decatur. You know it?'

'Yeah, I know it.'

'Pierre borrowed money from me and he's behind with the interest. He lives above the restaurant. Lean on him for me — point out that I take money seriously. I'll call you there.'

'Okay.'

Diamond dressed quickly, fed the cats and kissed Chelsea lightly. She stirred in her sleep but did not wake. He left the apartment, took the elevator to the underground garage and joined the traffic on Rampart. It took his Mustang twenty minutes to cross Royal and Chartres, then he wasted more time looking for a parking slot.

Eventually he locked the car and started walking. It was going to be another hot day. He turned into Decatur Street, passing tourists staring into the windows of art galleries. Above their heads, he saw a painted signboard, gilt-on-black:

PIERRE'S

He pushed through glass doors into the restaurant. A few people were taking coffee and beignets; it was still early for lunch, although a smell of seafood came from the kitchen. There was a smiling blonde girl at the cash desk and two waitresses near the serving door.

Pierre, in a dark suit, white shirt and plain black bowtie, moved between the tables checking spotless white cloths and gleaming silver. There were flowers on each table and it was obvious the place had been newly decorated, using the gilt-and-black motif. Nicely got up for the tourist trade, Diamond thought; Greco's money had been well spent.

Pierre was stockily built with short blond hair. His clean-shaven face had a solid jaw with eyes of a piercing quality.

Diamond didn't doubt that he could be tough when the situation demanded.

He moved towards the restauranteur and clamped a big black hand around his biceps, and squeezed. He kept his voice low.

'Let's go upstairs so we can talk in private. Mr. Greco will be phoning shortly.'

'I have nothing to say to you. Anything I need to say, I shall say directly to — '

Diamond's grip tightened till he saw Pierre wince; then, still gripping his arm, he led the way to the stairs at the back of the restaurant. They went up in silence. At the top was a landing and a door marked: *Private*.

'My family,' Pierre said. 'Leave them out of this. Please.'

'Of course. This is business, strictly business. Mr. Greco's a little worried about his money.'

Reluctantly, Pierre opened the door and Diamond hustled him through into the family's living quarters. The room was big and airy with a high ceiling, and the furnishings old but comfortable. A woman in a plain green dress was seated on a sofa with a girl of about six, listening to a cello sonata on the hi-fi.

'Annette, Yvonne,' Pierre said quietly. 'I want you both to go into the bedroom and shut the door. We have money matters to discuss.'

Diamond looked around the room, noting the position of windows and doors. He swung a hard-backed chair to him and straddled it, folding his arms over the wooden back.

The woman said quickly, 'Please don't move the furniture — my daughter's blind and needs to know where everything is.'

'I'm sorry to hear that,' Diamond said politely.

'A drink?' Pierre suggested.

'I don't use alcohol.'

'What is this?' Annette demanded suspiciously. 'Who are you?'

'I represent Mr. Greco.'

Annette gulped air into her lungs and made a sobbing sound. 'I warned you, Pierre,' she wailed. 'I warned you against that man!'

The little girl clutched at her mother's dress, suddenly scared. 'What is it, mama? What's happening? Please tell me.'

Annette made soothing noises, and Diamond said; 'Can we get down to it now? Mr. Greco will be phoning shortly and he'll want answers. Will you pay what you owe him?'

'I can't — not immediately,' Pierre said in a desperate voice. 'I'll pay, yes — every cent I owe. But I need more time.'

'Time is something you're running out of.'

'The delay is essential, I assure you. I've spent a lot of money on renovation downstairs — you saw for yourself. And my regular custom is building up nicely. Just now I need every cent I can scrape up to keep the business growing.'

Annette interrupted angrily. 'That man is too greedy. It's the rate of interest — it's much too high.'

'You should have thought of that before,' Diamond said mildly.

'All we need is a little more time — '

'Mr. Greco won't wait. He wants his interest now.'

'He wants, he wants,' Pierre said, clenching his hands. 'That's tough. He'll just have to — '

The telephone rang and Diamond turned down the hi-fi and reached for the receiver.

'Is he paying?' a neutral voice asked.

'He says he hasn't the money right now, and I'm inclined to believe him. He'll pay up if you give him time.'

'You can tell him I'll wait for the capital. It's the interest I'm concerned about, and I want it now. He pays all the back interest he owes and keeps paying interest — that's the name of the game. The longer he hangs on to the capital, the more money he owes me.' Leon Greco sighed softly. 'Convince him.'

Diamond turned to Annette and said, 'Maybe you and the little girl had better leave us.'

Annette came to her feet, her face set. 'I'm staying,' she said shrilly. 'You won't dare do anything to Pierre in front of me!'

The receiver crackled to life. 'Who's that you're talking to, Wash?'

'His wife and daughter are in the room.'

'Yeah? That's fine.' Greco raised his voice deliberately. 'This is what you'll do. Grab hold of that stupid cow he uses for a bed-warmer and smash her face to a pulp.'

'Keep your voice down,' Diamond said tersely. 'She can hear you.'

'So what? Say, I've just had a better idea.' Greco's raised voice boomed from the telephone and echoed through the room. 'You say their kid's there? Great! Break her wrists — both of them. Pierre will sure get the message that way.'

Greco's laughter made Diamond's flesh crawl. 'Goddamn it, a man doesn't hurt a kid!'

'You going soft on me? I pay you good money — now do what I tell you.'

Diamond started a slow count to five, holding his breath and looking at the blind girl as she clutched hold of her mother's dress. Pierre and Annette stared back at him.

'I just quit working for you,' he said, and put down the receiver and walked out of the room and down the stairs.

Out on the street he shook with a cold rage and took deep breaths till he felt calm enough to drive in city traffic. He got in his Mustang and circled back via Iberville to his condo.

When he let himself into his apartment, Chelsea was up and dressed, humming *Ain't Misbehavin'* as she prepared a meal.

'Pork chops with salad. All right with you, Wash?'

'Anything at all. I don't feel much like eating.'

Chelsea raised an eyebrow. 'How come, big boy? I've never known you to go off your food.'

'I quit the job.'

'Well, I'm glad. I never understood why you took it on in the first place. Greco isn't exactly my idea of a human being.'

Diamond paced up and down the kitchen, hands clenching and unclenching.

'Easy money, I guess. Nothing seemed to matter very much when I got back from 'Nam. I was sick of the mud and blood, the stupidity and killing. Life didn't seem worth two bits. Guess I wasn't feeling any too human myself. I knew Greco was in the rackets — so what? He paid more money than anyone else and that was at the head of my list.

'Leaning on a bunch of crooks didn't bother me any. I figured they deserved all they got. They were asking for it. But you know what he wanted me to do today? Damage a blind kid. Jesus, that's sick!'

He felt disgust with himself and his short laugh made a harsh sound like a dog barking.

'Maybe I'll get a bit of self-respect back now. Could be you've had a good effect on me.'

'So what are you going to use for bread?' Chelsea asked, her mind turning immediately to the practical issue. 'Can you afford to keep this place on?'

Diamond shrugged. 'I've enough in the bank not to worry for a while. Enough to buy time to look around.'

'Well, even if your middle name is Teagarden, you sure ain't going to make it as a horn player. You're good enough to sit in as an amateur, but you're not up to pro standard — and there's a lot of competition around.'

Chelsea frowned. 'And what's Greco going to do? He won't like one of his men walking out on him — bad for his image. He might even think he can't afford to let you get away with it.'

3

Pick-up on Basin Street

The damp heat was even worse inside the massage parlour than out on the street. Leon Greco, wearing a hand-cut grey suit that had cost nearly a thousand dollars, put up with it because he owned the place. And he knew that if he didn't check the books personally, Irene would cut herself an extra slice of the take.

The walls of the front office were used to advertise her services and included poster-sized colour pictures of the girls.

FRENCH, SWEDISH AND EBONY MASSAGE
Very personal attention by one of our many lovely girls.
Body Talk a Speciality of the House
VISITING MASSEUSES PROVIDED

Already Irene had tried to distract him

by offering one of the new masseusses, a bronzed teenager with pert breasts wearing flesh-coloured bikini briefs.

'You know by now that I never mix pleasure with business,' he said in a tone of mild disapproval.

Irene shrugged. She knew; that was why he was called the Fox. The parlour was registered in her name, so he was clean if ever the cops decided to clamp down.

She was a big-built woman with a long face framed by platinum hair, wearing a form-fitting black dress and black silk tights. 'Sometimes I think you only get your kicks from dollars and cents.'

Greco smiled and eased himself back from the desk and closed the accounts books. He pushed them to one side and lit a Cuban cigar.

'Looks okay.' he said. 'Just keep them that way, Irene.'

'Of course, Leon.'

Greco savoured his cigar, a slim man with small neatly-groomed hands and a grey silk tie resting on a developing paunch. His hair was beginning to thin

29

and the only big thing about him was the nose set in a pale face.

His thoughts revolved about Wash Diamond; how that crazy black had walked out on him. Stupid. He still couldn't quite believe it had happened. He paid top money to buy loyalty, and money meant he had absolute power over his people. They were things to be ordered around.

Something would have to be done to replace him. And he'd have to make the point that nobody — nobody — just walked away from his organization when it suited them.

He tapped ash from his cigar and glanced at Irene. 'Find Turk for me.'

Irene used her desk phone and, after the third call, said. 'He's at Oscar's.'

Perspiring, Greco rose to his feet and walked out of the massage parlour. He climbed into the back of a medium-sized grey Ford and relaxed in the chill of air-conditioning.

His personal bodyguard, Kenny, was at the wheel engrossed in a new girlie magazine. Kenny bought them all and his eyes were out on stalks, but this never interfered with his ability to draw a gun when needed. It had taken a while for Greco to appreciate this, but now he didn't let his chauffeur's over-riding interest in the female form bother him. It was something he could use.

'Oscar's,' he said.

Kenny nodded, slid his magazine — open to the centrefold — onto the seat beside him. He was a beanpole with sharp enough features to make him look like a hatchet-man.

He adjusted the gun bulging under his armpit and drove smoothly away.

It was a car that did not draw attention to itself. Greco exchanged his car every year for a new model; always the same make, nothing ostentatious, always with air-conditioning. He still had not adapted to the moist and sticky heat of Louisiana.

Kenny weaved through the traffic, babbling away to himself. He had only one thing on his mind.

'The new one at the Peep Show . . . Boy, she really does something for me . . . '

Sometimes Greco thought Kenny didn't know he was voicing his thoughts; he ran on as if his mouth were disconnected from his brain.

But Leon Greco had learnt to shut out the noise. At just on forty, he wasn't feeling as young as he was when he moved south from New York. There he had been strictly small-time. Here he'd done all right for himself, it hadn't proved difficult to organize the rackets and so bring himself to the top.

He leaned forward to stub out his cigar butt in the ashtray as Kenny cruised through the suburb of Metairie. It was time to think about pulling out, and he had an idea how to arrange that.

Beyond a row of tree-shaded houses, Kenny brought the Ford to a stop outside Oscar's Gymnasium. Greco crossed the sidewalk and went inside. The place smelt like all gyms everywhere, a combination of sweat and old leather and embrocation. A couple of youngsters sparred in the ring; there were metal lockers lining one wall, massage tables, a steam-box and exercise bikes.

Greco stood inside the door looking about him. He nodded to Oscar, five-feet-nothing with a bald head and broken nose.

Turk was working out with a punch-bag, slamming it with bare hands and scowling because he couldn't hurt it; the bag always bounced back at him. He was a heavyweight, big as an ox, with a reputation for dirty fighting. He wore an old sweatshirt and trunks.

Greco watched him for some minutes, then called softly: 'Turk.'

The fighter stopped punching and stepped back, peering about with small eyes close-set in a square head. He wasn't all that bright — just maybe Diamond had been too bright — but he could follow simple orders.

'Hi, Mr. Greco.' Turk's voice was a high squeak, the result of a right-hand smash to his voice-box; it sounded odd in so huge a man.

'Diamond retired. If you want his job, you've got it.'

Greed glittered in the pig eyes. More than once Turk had dropped a hint that he could take Diamond any day, and that the job should never have gone to him.

'I want.'

Greco said quietly, 'I can't allow Wash to walk out on me without leaving him a message. I'll give you his address. After that, I'll have another job for you.'

'Gee, thanks Mr. Greco.'

★   ★   ★

Diamond was walking the streets of the city, dropping in at different clubs to see if anyone wanted a horn player. He'd had no luck so far but was not feeling discouraged as he strode along Basin Street among the tourists studying price tags in shop windows. He was passing the St. Louis Cemetery No. 1, with its oven-like vaults and iron fences, when an old Plymouth drew into the curb, a door swung open and a voice said:

'Get in, feller.' Diamond looked carefully at the driver and saw a Panama hat that had seen better days perched atop a walnut-wrinkled face. The man's jacket was hanging loose to show a holstered Police Special.

'What's this about?'

'Just a few questions, boy. Now get in unless you want me to book you and haul your black ass down to the station.'

Diamond slid into the front passenger seat and slammed the door. The car edged out into the traffic flow.

'D'you have any identification?'

The driver showed his I.D., and growled, 'A real bright boy would have asked before he got in the car.'

'Well, Detective Cave, suppose you-all tell me what this is about. I'll have you know I'm busy job hunting.'

'Is that a fact?' Diamond heard the suspicion in Cave's tone. 'I heard you'd broken with the Fox.'

'Where'd you hear that, man? I'm telling you, I was never with him.'

'I'll check you out, feller, don't think I won't. If it's true, you're going to need a friend. What sort of job are you looking for?'

'Playing jazz horn, man.'

Cave snorted. 'Tom-toms for jungle

bunnies! Just so long as you don't call it music, and I don't have to listen.'

Diamond rolled his eyes and put on an Uncle Tom act. 'Did nobody ever tell you all this racist talk is bad now?'

'I'm old fashioned. Can't seem to break the habit.'

The car circled the Superdome and swung back towards Canal Street, overtaking a horse-drawn carriage with a black driver in a top hat and a group of sightseers. As he saw the Vieux Carré ahead Diamond was haunted by the image of a blind girl.

'How old-fashioned?' he asked. 'Pierre's, on Decatur, could do with some protection. He's got a wife and daughter.'

'Yeah? It's stupid to go to a loan shark,' Cave said, and pulled over to let Diamond out. 'You may be seeing me again, boy.'

As the Plymouth glided away, Diamond began to foot it home. He was no longer in the mood for chasing a job; he felt uneasy at being picked up by a cop after quitting Greco. Now he was exposed, without protection. What had the detective really been after? Well, there was no sense in worrying about it; probably he'd never see him again.

He reached his condo and went up in the elevator. The door of his apartment was open and the manager stood in the doorway, staring in; he appeared disturbed by what he saw.

Diamond quickened his step, knowing Chelsea would not have left the door open. Then he saw that the lock had been smashed.

'What happened?'

'I had a complaint about the noise in your apartment.' The manager had a fussy manner and shoulder-length hair; he waved manicured fingers at the interior.

Diamond stepped past him and stopped dead. It was immediately obvious the wreckers had called. His collection of jazz records — some of them rare items — had been tipped onto the carpet and stamped on. His books had been ripped apart and the pages scattered.

He moved quickly around the apartment. His trumpet had been ruined; the tube wrenched out of shape and the valves snapped off. In the bathroom he smelt burnt paper; the tub was filled with charred music scores.

He went into the kitchen and what he saw there made his stomach turn sour. Ginger and her two kittens had been gutted with a carving knife; the floor was stained with their blood. Diamond's hands knotted and he felt cold; suppose Chelsea had been here?

It had to be Greco, he thought. She had been right after all. Greco had felt he must hit back.

Standing in the doorway, the manager flapped his hands. 'This cannot be tolerated,' he said, his expression suggesting he might be chewing on a cockroach. 'I insist that you leave immediately, Mr. Diamond. I simply cannot allow this sort of thing to happen in my building.'

4

Peeper

Turk felt good as he jog-trotted through the suburbs on Highway Sixty-one, heading out of the city. He flexed his muscles and practised deep breathing, in no hurry for the night's work.

He was now Leon Greco's enforcer, and proud of it. Diamond was out. He had some regret that the big spade hadn't been home when he'd paid his visit, but he'd get the message all right.

The sky flamed with sunset and lights winked on in the windows of apartment blocks and neat rows of houses as darkness grew long shadows. Cars swished by.

Well, Muller would be on the job for sure and that gave him an anticipatory thrill. There was nothing Turk liked better than beating up a small guy, and this one was going to suffer. Mr. Greco said he'd been helping himself to the profits and Turk thought anyone who did that was stupid. Mr. Greco paid better than anybody — so Muller had to be taught to behave.

Turk was wearing a tracksuit, the evening was warm and sweat trickled from his armpits. He wiped his hands down his side, not wanting them to slip when he moved into action.

A glare of neon showed ahead, just off the highway, and he screwed up his eyes to read the sign:

MULLER'S USED CAR LOT
Auto Parts

He slowed his pace to take a careful look around. The one thing he didn't need now was a bunch of witnesses.

But Muller's place didn't appear to be busy and, behind the brilliant light of the showroom, was a patch of darkness. There were rows of used cars parked out front, each one gleaming with fresh polish. At the back were the wrecks, dismantled for spare parts, and hundreds of remoulded tyres in great piles.

Muller did all kinds of jobs for the rackets; disposed of hot items, provided a quick respray and false plates for stolen vehicles, and arranged unregistered cars when needed.

As Turk approached the office he saw Muller chatting up the help, a nice-looking broad. Robert Muller was young and fair-haired with a smile that showed his perfect teeth. He acted as though he were super-salesman of the year, and dressed in creased slacks, a white shirt and tie.

Turk walked through the doorway and Muller came to greet him, smiling, offering his hand.

'Can I help you, sir?'

Turk kicked his kneecap, disabling him and bringing tears to his eyes. He gripped Muller by the arms and hauled him outside, pausing in the doorway to call back in a high-pitched squeak: 'Better get an ambulance, honey. Your boss just met with an accident.'

He pushed Muller ahead of him, out of the bright lights and down a dark alley between towering stacks of tyres. He was grinning with anticipation. The area behind the office was huge, crammed with rusting wrecks and piles of spare parts; lamps, wheels, radios and batteries from a score of different models. The whole place looked like a scrap dump.

Muller hobbled along, pleading, 'I'm not going to make trouble — I'll give you my wallet — just don't hurt me any more.'

Turk forced him into deep shadow. 'You've got it all wrong, bud. I'm here on Mr. Greco's orders, and he said to work you over some.'

He squinted into the gloom, picked up an iron bar that had broken off a chassis and hefted it in his hand.

Muller moaned, 'Don't . . . please . . . '

Turk swung the bar viciously, connecting with Muller's already damaged knee-cap and smashing it. Muller screamed and fell down, rolling in agony on the ground, holding his knee and crying.

Turk used his foot to push him onto his back and hold him still. Then he swung the iron bar again, splintering in the bone of his other kneecap. Muller's shriek reached a new crescendo.

Turk tossed the iron bar aside and strolled away. He could still hear Muller screaming like a demented tomcat when he reached the highway and began a slow jogtrot as an ambulance drew up outside the front office.

★   ★   ★

Diamond was striding east along Rampart Street, on his way to Chelsea's apartment, when the Plymouth pulled up beside him.

Detective Cave said, 'Hop in, feller, and I'll give you a lift.'

'You again,' Diamond grunted, and hesitated.

Cave's voice turned sour. 'Get in for Christ's sake — I'm doing you a favour.'

Diamond shrugged and slid into the passenger seat. 'Esplanade Avenue, since you're running a taxi service.'

Cave took the car out into the traffic. 'I've been busy checking you out and it looks like your quitting Greco was the real thing . . . So, you got a job lined up? A place to live?'

'Not so far.'

'Well, I'm offering you a job. An honest job, okay?'

'I'm listening.'

Cave detoured to avoid a traffic jam. He lit a cigarette, his pale blue eyes glittering like chips of ice.

'I've been a detective for more than twenty years and I'm telling you I'm sick of the job. Times past you could nail some crook and make it stick — today, the germs have got rights, for Christ's sake! Pull in a mugger who bashes an old lady for her pension and the bleeding-heart liberals scream he's a victim of circumstances . . . with never a thought for the real victim.'

Cave started to cough and flipped his half-smoked Marlboro through the open window.

'It's all rehabilitation these days. If some low-life cops a sentence, he's out on parole before we've filed the paperwork. We're told they're misfits, deprived. Unless he's a bigshot — like your old pal

Greco — with a high-powered lawyer. Then he doesn't get to spend the night in jail because he's out on bail.'

'And if anyone shoots a cop, the killer is excused and protected and the do-gooders wave banners and scream police victimization. It makes me want to puke. I hate the scumbags.'

Diamond kept his face blank, watching the tourists inspect the artists' paintings on the iron railings in Jackson Square.

Cave asked, 'D'you reckon Greco is misunderstood?'

'Reckon he's real mean.'

'Yeah, I heard someone paid a visit to your pad. Turk's his enforcer now — he had a go at Muller last night. You'll need to watch out for that chippie of yours.'

Diamond bared his teeth and laid a black hand on the detective's arm. 'Use that word once more about Chelsea and I'll squash you as I would a bug.'

Cave glanced sideways at him. 'I believe you would at that — you're sure big enough. No offense meant.'

Diamond removed his hand and Cave went on: 'As I said, I checked you out.

And you ain't no Louis Armstrong is what I heard. Looked up your army record, and that's good. So what I'm prepared to do is fix you up as a private investigator — get you a license and a gun. That will give you some legal backing if Greco has a go at your girlfriend. Okay?'

Diamond was startled, then thoughtful. Finally, he nodded. 'I like it . . . except I know nothing about investigating.'

Cave turned the wheel and the car moved into Esplanade Avenue, and began to slow down.

'It's mostly observation. You keep your eyes open. You ask questions. You listen — everybody loves a good listener. If you do this full-time, you'll be surprised how much you learn.'

'Surprised is right,' Diamond said dryly. 'Do I make money, too?'

'Charge a daily rate. A century would be reasonable, but you can bump it up if you hook a rich client — and expenses, of course. Keep records. And always ask for a retainer so you aren't left holding an empty hat.'

Cave pulled in at the curb and stopped. 'So how about it?'

'You have a deal.'

'Fine. I'll need a photograph for the license.'

Diamond looked through his wallet. 'This do?'

Cave nodded. 'I'll fix it.'

Diamond climbed out onto the sunlit street and Cave drove away. Chelsea's apartment was in an old two-storey building and the stairs creaked as he went up. He rang the bell and she unlocked the door and opened it on a chain.

'It's me, Wash.'

Chelsea unchained and let him in. 'You see, I am being careful since you phoned.'

'That's good. Better safe than sliced.'

'Are you going to move in?'

Diamond shook his head. 'No way, baby — that could be dangerous for you.'

'Overnight then, till you find somewhere.'

'Yeah, I'll accept that. Greco isn't likely to move right now, because he'll expect me to have my guard up. And maybe he'll figure he's done enough and not bother any more.'

He picked his favourite chair and relaxed while Chelsea set the coffee percolating in the kitchen. Her apartment was smaller and cheaper and her housekeeping offhand; but it was bright with orange curtains and maroon rugs and bean cushions. Jazz magazines and records out of their sleeves were scattered in casual chaos. He always had to make an effort to stop himself straightening up after her.

When she joined him again, he told her about his second meeting with the white detective.

She pursed her lips. 'Don't trust that honky, Wash — he's up to something.'

'That figures. But a legal gun — why not?'

Chelsea sipped hot coffee. 'I'm sorry about your cats. You know I wasn't keen on them, but what Greco did was nasty. Anyway, I bought you a present.'

She went into the bedroom and returned holding a brass trumpet. 'It was cheap, at a pawnshop — but at least you can blow music again.'

'That's great!'

Diamond set down his mug and came to his feet. He took the horn and fingered the valves; they'd need some work done on them. He lifted the mouthpiece to his lips as Chelsea put on a record of *Rockin' Chair Blues*, blew a few notes experimentally, then joined in the chorus. When the record stopped, he hugged her.

'Thanks, baby. That's the best present I ever had — it really gives me a lift. Now let's make music together.'

★　★　★

The telephone was ringing.

Chelsea swore and, still half-asleep, groped blindly for the bedside table. She knocked over a water bottle and broke a glass and swore again. Finally she found the receiver.

'D'you know what time it is?' she screamed into the mouthpiece. 'It's the middle of the night!'

'I had my breakfast a couple of hours since.'

Chelsea thumped Diamond on the shoulder and he came awake immediately. 'Your detective,' she mumbled, and stuck her head under the pillow.

Diamond took the receiver from her and said, 'Hello.'

'Hope I wasn't interrupting anything. I've got your license, and fixed an office. Meet me outside the COIN-OP laundromat on Orleans.'

Cave cut off and Diamond swung his legs out of bed.

Chelsea muttered, 'He's setting you up, Wash,' and went back to sleep.

Diamond took a quick shower and dressed and left her apartment. He rode west along Royal, past antique shops, to Orleans Avenue. His stomach started rumbling when he came to a coffee bar; breakfast would have to wait.

He wondered what Cave was up to. The Jim Crow attitude wasn't as strong now that industrialisation had reached the city; but that didn't mean a white cop had to go out of his way to help a black man.

He recognized the Plymouth parked beneath a sign:

COIN-OP
Laundromat
The place was busy with young mothers with kids, and bachelors watching their wash go around in the big tubs.

Cave got out of his car carrying a small suitcase. 'Some people get up in the morning,' he said, and nodded towards a side door. A narrow flight of stairs led up to a landing and a single door. Hand-painted on pebbled glass was:

WASHINGTON T. DIAMOND
Investigations

Diamond stared blankly, then felt a stirring of pride. Beyond the door was a cubical office fitted with an ancient desk, swivel chair and a couple of cane chairs. There was a telephone, a battered green filing cabinet and a water cooler.

Another door led to a second room at the back, furnished with a single bed, shower and mini-kitchen.

'Guess you can rough it here for a while,' Cave said, watching him closely.

Diamond was amazed. 'How come

you've got everything fixed so fast?'

'Influence. It's one of those places we use when the Department needs an undercover house.'

Cave took a brand new plastic I.D. from his own jacket pocket and flipped it open. Diamond looked at his own photograph and personal details under the heading: *Licensed Private Investigator.*

Cave placed his suitcase on the desk and opened it. He brought out a revolver in a shoulder holster and two boxes of cartridges.

'You can use this, I guess?'

'I've seen a few guns before.'

'Maybe I can arrange for you to use our practice range later on. So all you need are clients, and maybe I can push a few of those your way.' Cave closed the case with a snap and gave a tight smile. 'I've placed an ad in the *Times-Picayune* and that should be appearing tomorrow. You can get a listing in Yellow Pages next issue.'

Diamond said, after a pause. 'Why are you doing all this? What d'you get out of it?'

Cave turned pale blue eyes on him, cold and hard as marbles.

'Don't look a gift horse in the mouth, feller. Just be grateful I'm setting you up in business.'

5

Black and Blue Client

Leon Greco relaxed in the cool comfort of his air-conditioned Ford. Some day, he thought, it would be nice to have a home of his own. Since his arrival in the big time, he seemed to relax only in the back of his car. He spent an hour each day in one or other of his many scattered offices, and in the bedrooms of available women, but otherwise he was always on the move. And his visits had to vary as to time and route.

He enjoyed his cigar as Kenny, babbling away about some stripper, drove him towards the airport. Both Wash and Muller had been dealt with and Turk seemed to be working out. Play this meeting right and he had an opening to a new life; it was time to withdraw from the rackets — with a safe line to provide plenty of cash.

Kenny turned off the highway and slid into a parking slot as close to the terminal buildings as he could get. As Greco opened the door and got out, the roar of jet engines swamped him. There was a bustle of electric trolleys and uniformed personnel and passengers. A plane took off, sweeping a dark shadow across the sun.

'Anything you want, Mr. Greco?'

'Not right now, Kenny.' He lifted his voice. 'I may be back tonight — if not, in the morning. I'll phone my time of arrival.'

He stood motionless, watching Kenny drive away, and feeling exposed. It was a long time since he'd gone anywhere without a bodyguard. In some ways — like now, when he needed privacy — Kenny could be a liability.

He shrugged off his mood, crossed to the ticket office and bought a return flight to Houston. He bought a copy of the local paper, checked his boarding gate and walked through towards the waiting aircraft.

Since NASA had opened a place in

New Orleans, the short hop was routine. More important, the meeting was off his home ground. He boarded, fastened his seatbelt and, when the hostess came round, kept his gaze on the *Times-Picayune*. He wasn't looking for attention; he preferred to go unnoticed.

The plane took off, climbing steadily into a clear blue sky. Slowly, Lake Pontchartrain shrank to a puddle, the Mississippi wound its tortuous way inland and the Gulf of Mexico expanded to a blue-green horizon. He accepted one drink; not to do so would attract attention, but he nursed it throughout the flight.

He needed a clear head to cope with Madden. An assumed name, of course; but he was aware of the reputation behind the name.

The flight seemed over almost as soon as it started and the plane glided in to make a smooth landing. He went down the passenger steps and walked towards the terminal building; a clock above the newsstand told him he was on time. He used the escalator to reach the observation deck, glanced around and saw nobody he recognised — just families watching aircraft take-off and land.

There was a strong smell of jet fuel in the air, which vibrated with engine noise. Madden knew what he was doing, arranging to meet in the open; they could see everyone and nobody could hear what was said.

He felt suddenly, unaccountably nervous. It was ridiculous; he couldn't remember the last time he'd felt this way, but then his whole future depended on the meeting going right.

He folded his newspaper with the title outside.

A man approached from the top of the escalator, also carrying a newspaper folded so he could read the name: *New York Herald*. He was about thirty, freshly shaven, with a smell of Cologne and barbered shoulder-length hair. His suit was obviously expensive and discreetly dark. He looked completely self-possessed, a typical up-and-coming executive on his way to the boardroom.

Cool grey eyes observed the *Times-Picayune*. 'Mr. Greco?'

'Yes. Mr. Madden?'

The younger man nodded and, together, they moved to an isolated part of the observation deck and leaned on the safety rail. They looked out across the airport and watched a Boeing lift off. The air throbbed with noise, deafening them for minutes, and there was no one else anywhere near.

Madden, too, was on neutral territory, the risk to either man minimal. They put their heads close so they could hear each other.

Madden had a Northern accent, clipped and precise. 'I need a team putting together down here. Can you handle that for me?'

'I've got contacts. What kind of team do you have in mind?'

'Three strong-arms. Two drivers.'

'I can arrange it. How much?'

Madden gave him an appraising glance. 'Ten per cent of the take is usual.'

'Agreed. How long do I have to find them?'

'Take your time. Everything has to be just right before I make a move. I want real cool men, no hotheads, no kids out to prove themselves. And make it clear that no one carries a gun on this job.'

'I'll see you get the best. I'll call you when I've got your team lined up.'

'Good enough.' Madden nodded casually, and moved away.

Greco took particular care not to watch which flight Madden left on. He didn't want to know, and wanted any hidden observer to be sure of that fact. He phoned a message to be relayed to Kenny to pick him up.

While he waited for a flight back to New Orleans, he reviewed likely men for Madden's job. He was going to be particular. He felt excited for the first time in years. Madden was a top organiser and, if this went right, word would soon get around that Leon Greco could be relied on. Then he'd be asked by other organisers to provide teams of specialists, and he would quickly build a thriving — and safe — business.

Diamond leaned back in a swivel chair, his feet crossed on the desktop. He held a glass of iced water in one hand and there was a broad smile on his chocolate face as he contemplated his name in reverse on the pebbled-glass door. The window was open, bringing the sounds of washing machines below and an appetising smell of gumbo from next door, a murmur of voices as tourists passed by on the sidewalk.

His thoughts drifted and he wondered what a private eye was supposed to do while waiting for a client to arrive. Earlier, he'd spent a couple of hours working out at a gym, had lunch and completed two dozen lengths in a swimming pool.

The heat was slowly getting to him and he was about ready to doze off when footfalls tapped on the wooden stairs.

He removed his feet from the desk, grabbed a note-pad and ball-pen and tried to look alert as the door opened and a woman walked in.

Diamond smiled as he rose to greet her.

She was black and carried a copy of the local paper open to the advertisement Cave had placed. 'You Diamond?'

He noted a plain gold ring on her finger. 'Yes ma'am. How can I help you?'

She took her time looking him over, seemed impressed, and sat in a cane chair across the desk.

Diamond resumed his seat. She was in her middle twenties, he judged, a ripe beauty wearing a bright blue dress tight enough to show off her figure. Her face was marked, cheeks bruised and lips split.

'Mrs. — ?'

'Call me Louise.'

'Louise is fine, ma'am. You want to tell me your trouble?'

For a moment she looked as though she might burst into tears; so her pride had been hurt too. Then she regained control.

'It's my husband, Melvin.'

Her voice was so low he had to strain to hear. Then she raised her voice and stated clearly: 'I purely love that man, and the only thing I've got against him is he beats me when he's drunk. And he's drunk too damned often!'

Her eyes measured his size.

'You figure you might throw a scare into him — you're big enough, I reckon — scare him off drinking, for a hundred bucks? You can take the dough off him. It's like, I don't want to lose Melvin, but I sure can't take any more drinking and beating up on me. Can you make that clear to him?'

'I can try,' Diamond said mildly. 'A woman should be treated right by her man.'

'I don't want him hurt none,' Louise said quickly.

Washington T. Diamond stood up behind his desk, his face solemn. He had his first case.

'I might just dust him down a little,' he admitted.

They went downstairs to his car and he drove north to Louise's place, part of a housing development just above Basin Street. The apartment was neat and clean, and she brewed coffee and chicory while they waited for Melvin to get home from work. Louise switched the radio to her favourite soap opera while Diamond thought how he might handle the situation.

Louise looked at the electric wall clock. 'Melvin'll be maybe ten minutes,' she said nervously.

'Do you have any whisky?'

She jumped up. 'I should have asked if — '

Diamond shook his head. 'I don't drink. It's just to set the scene a little. A couple of glasses and — if you don't mind — could you slip into a wrap and let your hair down? The idea is to give him something to worry about.'

Louise's eyes sparkled. 'Yeah, I like it.'

She went into the bedroom and came back in a wrap that showed a lot of bare leg and the cleft between her breasts. She brought a tray from the kitchen with a whisky bottle and two glasses, and half-filled the glasses.

She took a sip, and giggled. 'Maybe it's a good thing Melvin is due home, Mr. Diamond!'

He relaxed as she lit a cigarette and plumped herself down on the couch beside him and mussed the cushions.

'Maybe it is,' he said dryly. 'Just don't overdo it, or I might have a real fight on my hands.'

A door slammed and a voice called, 'You cooking, Louise? Hurry it, will ya? I've got a drinking date with some buddies — sure ain't got no time to waste.'

A lean negro appeared in the doorway, a flashy dresser, handsome with a neat moustache. He saw Diamond, stopped in his tracks and scowled.

'Who're you, man? What you think you're doing with my wife?'

He sniffed whisky fumes and stared hard at Louise's gaping wrap. 'I'm telling you, I don't like what I see here.'

Diamond rose and stretched, towering over Melvin. 'I'm a friend of Louise's, a friend you owe some money.'

He took a step forward, opening big hands and putting on a frightening face.

'Say, what is this?'

Louise blew a smoke ring and crushed

out her cigarette, shaking with excitement.

Diamond lifted Melvin easily so his toes left the floor, and jerked a wallet from his inside jacket pocket. He dumped Melvin, counted off a hundred dollars and tossed the wallet back. There wasn't much left in it.

'Hey, man,' Melvin protested. 'That's my drinking money!'

Diamond shook his head sadly. 'No way, Melvin. You just quit drinking, so you don't need the dough. You beat up Louise when you drink, so I'm helping you to stop, get it?'

Melvin was outraged. 'Who says I beat her?'

'Her face says so.'

Melvin looked at his wife as if he hadn't seen her before, and moistened his lips. 'Hell, maybe — I don't rightly know what I'm doing when I've had a few. You know how it is.'

'Yeah, I know. And you know a man doesn't beat up a fine wife like yours and still keep her. So that makes me your best friend. You've got a real loving woman there, so why don't you hit the sack and show her a good time before someone else does.'

Diamond picked up Melvin again and shook him the way a dog takes a rat in its teeth and shakes it.

'Just remember, Louise has got plenty of friends. You hit her once more and I'll break you in two.'

Diamond dropped him like a sack of potatoes on the couch, and Louise moved in to console her husband. He grinned to himself as he went out through the door.

★   ★   ★

Kenny was waiting with the Ford when Leon Greco landed and sucked in a lungful of steamy New Orleans' air. The Fox moved swiftly to the car and got in the back, grateful for the air-conditioning.

'Good trip, Mr. Greco?' Kenny asked, putting away the girlie magazine he had been studying.

'Fine, just fine.'

He was in a good mood, pleased with life and the way things were working out for him. He lit a cigar as the car edged out into the traffic and headed towards the city centre.

Kenny's lips moved incessantly as he drove. 'That Go-go dancer . . . '

When he got the car where he wanted it, he interrupted his unconscious babbling long enough to say; 'Jacobs was on the blower while you were away. He left this message — 'What you suspected is a fact'. He said you'd understand.'

Greco chewed the end of his cigar, spoiling it. His good mood was spoilt too. He mashed his butt into the Ford's ashtray.

He understood what Jacobs meant all right. For a while now he'd suspected that Roach, who managed the video porn factory, was into him for a sizable slice of dough. It was easy enough; all he had to do was run off a few extra copies and sell them privately.

Greco expected this and was prepared to allow it on a small scale. But it seemed that Roach was ambitious. He was scaling up his operation till it cut into Greco's own profits.

Jacobs, his accountant, had been probing the situation and now confirmed it, so . . .

I can do without this, Leon Greco thought, and I'll goddamn well put a stop to it.

He peered through the window. Looming ahead was the huge white oval of the Superdome.

He leaned forward and spoke to Kenny. 'Stop at the Post Office. I need a public call box to give Turk instructions.'

6

Bodyguard

'This is a hell of a small room,' Chelsea complained. 'It's a pity you're so damn big — there's hardly room for you, never mind me as well.'

Diamond grinned broadly. 'Always room for you, baby.'

He had his coat off and shirtsleeves rolled up. With Chelsea's help, he'd cleaned the room behind his office, cleared out his belongings from the condominium and dumped most of them at her place. They'd been shopping and stocked the tiny fridge. Now she was intent on turning the back room into a temporary home.

It was small, Diamond admitted, but it had a bed and a closet for clothes, an electric stove and a shower. It would do till he found himself an apartment.

Chelsea pushed back a straggling hair

as she scrubbed the sink. 'Well, there's no more excuses for dirty shirts,' she said. 'Not with a laundromat right below.'

'And I shan't starve next door to a gumbo restaurant — '

When the phone rang in the office, Chelsea went through and answered. 'Diamond Investigations.'

A familiar voice said, apparently amused: 'Got himself a secretary, has he? Let me speak to the big feller.'

Chelsea handed the phone to Diamond, murmuring, 'It's that detective again.'

Cave said, 'You have a client on his way, and he needs a bodyguard. You'll understand when you hear what he's got to say.'

Cave rang off abruptly, and Diamond rolled down his shirtsleeves and put on his jacket.

Chelsea removed her overall and tidied her hair. 'With a client arriving, it'll look better if you have a secretary. I'll stay till he arrives, okay?'

'If you say so.'

She made fresh coffee and they relaxed

70

till footfalls sounded on the stairs. Then she went into the office and waited behind the desk.

The man who entered was olive-skinned and wore sharp clothes with a Fu Manchu moustache and sideboards; his gaze travelled up and down Chelsea's figure as if he'd had a lot of practice.

'My name's Roach,' he said, and showed his teeth in a wolfish smile. 'Any time you want to make some extra money, I can arrange it.'

She kept her temper for Wash's sake. 'If you'll just take a seat, Mr. Roach, I'll inform Mr. Diamond that you're here.'

She went into the back room and closed the door. 'Name's Roach, and he's a creep. You know him?'

'I've heard the name somewhere.'

Chelsea left for an appointment with her hairdresser and Diamond stepped into his office and shook hands with Roach. He saw a bony man in a tight-fitting blue-stripe, a tie starring a fluorescent nude and two-tone shoes.

As Diamond seated himself at his desk,

Roach said chattily: 'Nice looking secretary bird you've got there.'

Diamond forced himself to remember this man was a client and just nodded.

Roach looked carefully at the size of him. 'I don't think we ever met, but I'm sure glad you split with Greco.'

'We had a difference of opinion.'

Roach grinned and his mouthful of teeth reminded Diamond of a shark. He seated himself in a cane chair, carefully adjusting his pants so as not to spoil the crease and crossed his legs. He appeared completely relaxed.

'So I can fight fire with fire. The Fox had Jacobs investigating me so, next thing, his new enforcer will be calling.' He paused. 'You know I'm running his porn factory for him? I'm going to need protection — keep me in one piece and I'll pay top rate. You interested?'

What was it Cave had said? 'Turk's his enforcer now'. And Cave had pushed this porn merchant his way, putting him in the middle. Why?

Roach took out a wallet stuffed with notes. He peeled off ten and spread them out on the desktop like a hand of cards. 'Ten centuries, okay?'

Diamond looked at the money, one thousand bucks' worth of protection. Someone — Turk? — had cut up his cats and ruined his gear; someone was going to pay for that. Yet he felt suspicious of Roach. He looked scared, but not scared enough for a bony man with a bone-breaker after him. There was something he was holding back.

Diamond scooped up the money, folded it and put it away. 'Yeah,' he said. 'I'm interested.'

He stepped into the back room and strapped on the shoulder holster, adjusted his jacket so it wasn't obvious. They went downstairs to Roach's car and headed south, past the St. Louis Cathedral with its three steeples, to the waterfront.

Roach drove towards Canal Street, passing ships being unloaded, tall cranes and trucks. The factory had been a warehouse at one time. Diamond had never been inside, though he'd heard this was one more racket Greco was into. The building was big and old, given a lick of paint on the outside and a plastic nameplate proclaiming:

ROACH VIDEO

They went through an open gate and across a yard. The interior was as big and as high as an aircraft hangar. Along one wall were assembly benches with young girls on high stools putting the finished tapes into boxes ready for despatch. The floor was cement, the lighting fluorescent.

Opposite was a production line for videotape copying; one machine played the master tape and a bank of slave machines each recorded a copy. There was a white-coated technician supervising.

Roach gestured with his hand. 'We're only concerned with copying here. The master comes from a studio specializing in hard-core porn. And it's the real stuff, no faking. I can give you a copy of our latest if you want.'

'No thanks,' Diamond said, looking around.

At the back of the warehouse, an

overalled man loaded finished tapes into a delivery van. There was a small office with filing cabinets and a typist.

'I've got an apartment upstairs,' Roach said, leading the way up a flight of stairs beside the office.

It was a comfortable apartment, luxuriously furnished and equipped with video equipment and a stack of tapes. It looked from the raunchy titles as though Roach probably enjoyed his work.

Diamond checked a door opening onto a fire escape. 'Keep it bolted,' he advised, 'and get a chain for your apartment door. Don't make it easy for anyone to reach you.'

Roach nodded, not really interested. 'I've got some work to do in the office. You coming?'

They went downstairs, and Roach used the phone to arrange transport. He looked at the wall clock.

'I'm taking lunch here today. Okay with you?'

'That's best.'

Roach sent his office girl for food for them both and Diamond inspected the factory. There were two ways in; the front entrance across the yard and the loading bay at the rear — but only one door to Roach's office.

After a quick lunch — hamburgers with French fries and milk shakes — Diamond borrowed a chair and placed it where he could watch both entrances and settled down to wait.

The afternoon was hot and drowsy. Roach kept busy, moving between his office and the bank of video machines. At five o'clock, the factory shut down and the workers left.

Diamond got up, stretched, and walked about. Any tine now, he thought; or would Turk wait for darkness? He made sure the rear door was locked and kept watch on the yard.

An hour passed quietly; then a bulky figure wearing a tracksuit jogged through the gate.

Diamond recognized Turk's square head as he came towards the factory entrance. He was big all right, and Diamond had heard he was a dirty fighter. He moved easily, flexing his muscles, grinning lazily.

Diamond called to Roach, in his office. 'Turk's here. You stay put — I'll handle this.'

He stepped out of the doorway, into the yard to give himself room to move. Turk saw him, slowed to a stop, his small eyes blinking rapidly. His high tinny voice sounded plaintive: 'What're you doing here, Wash?'

They faced each other in the empty yard, the silence broken only by the siren of a tug on the river, two big men — one white and one black — and Diamond eager to fight.

'Stopping you getting to Roach.'

Turk seemed confused. His orders were to cripple Roach; the Fox hadn't said any thing about Diamond. 'Mr. Greco — '

'I don't work for Greco. Right now I work for Roach. D'you think you can get past me?'

Turk was slow on the uptake. 'You're interfering,' he complained. 'Mr. Greco won't like that.'

'I suggest you tell that honky bastard to leave us alone then.'

Turk began to move around Diamond, who shifted his position to stay between the enforcer and his victim.

'You're in my way, Wash.'

'And that's right where I'm staying. D'you know anything about my cats? If you do, you can guess what I'll do to you.'

'Roach is a crook, you know that. He's got to learn he can't rob Mr. Greco.'

'Greco is a crook!'

Somewhere in the background, Roach laughed.

Turk hesitated, frustrated because he couldn't easily get at his victim. He looked past Diamond, to the shadowy figure in the doorway, and raised his voice.

'I'll be coming back for you, Roach. Don't think I won't — you can't hide for long. And then I'll take you apart.'

Diamond dipped his hand under his jacket, brought out his gun and levelled it.

'I've got a P.I's license now, and you'll have me to deal with if you show your face again. I can take you out any time — legally. And get away with it.'

Turk stared into the black hole in the

barrel of Diamond's revolver, and didn't like it. His sweat turned clammy and he backed away; no one had said anything about facing a gun.

He kept going till he reached the gate, then turned about and jog-trotted out of the yard. He called back, 'You ain't getting away with nothing, Wash. We'll see you off.'

He put on a spurt until he felt himself out of range of the revolver, then hunted for a call box. It took several calls and most of his small change to track down Leon Greco.

When he finally got through, his boss sounded exasperated.

'What the hell's Wash up to, guarding a creep like Roach?' And, you — are you scared of him or something? What do you think I pay you for? Have I got to do everything myself?'

Turk said, in a small squeaky voice, 'He's got a gun, Mr. Greco.'

'So what?' Greco sighed into the mouthpiece. 'Okay, I'll send Kenny to take his gun away if it bothers you that much. Then you take that goddamn

Roach apart, limb from limb, and make sure it hurts. The nerve of that crumb, hiring one of my men to look out for him. Treat him rough — I'll put someone else in to run the business.'

7

Rip-Off

Fred Cave sat in his Plymouth, which was parked just off Bourbon, looking along the street. His wrinkled face wore a sour smile as he wondered how Diamond was making out between Roach and Turk. Maybe something would come of it, maybe not; he could only wait and see. Cave had a lot of patience when it came to getting at Leon Greco.

It was early evening and, over one doorway, a sign in winking neon attracted his attention:

PEEP SHOW
Live Models!

He watched men enter and leave; it was a new place just opened and he suspected that Greco might have an interest in it.

He left his car and strolled along to the doorway. A notice proclaimed:

One Price
Five dollars — five minutes

He went inside and saw a row of peepholes and men of all shapes and ages staring through them. Just inside the door, the manager was taking money. He was thin with a gold tooth and pimples.

He took one look at Cave and smelt cop. 'Free to you, Officer. Enjoy.' He waved a hand towards a vacant slot.

Cave crossed to the glassed slit and peered through. The back room was lighted by a shaded red lamp to simulate the warmth and privacy of a bedroom. There were three young girls on view; one naked on the wide bed. They shot sly glances at the peepholes and giggled amongst themselves and looked more scared than provocative.

Cave turned back to the manager. 'How old are those girls, for Christ's sake?'

'Old enough.'

'College girls, if that,' Cave said, disgusted. 'School kids! I'm busting you right now. Turn everyone out and lock up.'

The manager stared at him, then put his hand in his pocket. 'Two hundred bucks, okay?'

Cave looked coldly at him. 'You can tell Greco there's one cop who won't take his money. Now shut down — and see those kids get home all right.'

★   ★   ★

After Turk had left the video factory, Roach came out, laughing and stroking his moustache. Diamond decided he looked more than ever like Fu Manchu.

'You handled that just right,' he said, and then became serious. 'I'll be staying late tonight — I've got some stuff to sort out that I'm expecting transport to pick up. It'll be okay if you just stick around the yard.'

Diamond nodded, wondering why Roach seemed unperturbed; he must have heard Turk's threat to return. And this time, he might well have reinforcements.

'I'll watch the yard entrance — it's not likely that anyone will show till after dark now.'

Roach went back inside, took off his jacket and turned on the lights, including the yard light. It was quiet with everyone else gone; only the two of them were left on the factory site.

Diamond pulled up a chair and rested easy, watching shadows gather in the twilight. River sounds came to him as he sat just inside the doorway, near the time-clock, looking out. Behind him he could hear Roach whistling an oldie from *Oklahoma* as he worked; there didn't seem to be anything wrong with his nerves. Mechanical noises echoed in the stillness, and it sounded as though he were dismantling some equipment.

The time-clock ticked loudly in Diamond's ear. It began to seem that the biggest part of an investigator job was just waiting around. Like the army, he thought; a brief spell of action and then more waiting around until the next bout of action. He smiled at the thought.

Maybe if he'd spent more time with the brass band and less with the basketball team at his A and M University, he'd have made the grade as a jazz musician. And maybe not . . . he'd wasted too much time on manual jobs — truck-driving to road-making, building his muscles before he volunteered for the army to get away from the South.

The whine of a car engine sliced through the night. It was coming nearer; headlights threw a beam across the gate and went out. The dark shape of a car turned into the yard, reversed, and parked facing outwards. The engine switched off.

Two figures emerged; one a great hulking shadow that had to be Turk. The other tall and thin; Kenny, Diamond guessed.

He rose from the chair and called into the factory: 'They're here — get under cover.'

Turk and Kenny moved quickly towards the door and, suddenly, there was a gun in Kenny's hand.

'Stand still, spade, while Turk here has a little chat with your client.'

Diamond watched Kenny's gun hand, working out angles of fire. Turk came directly towards him, grinning; he had to pass close to get through the door to reach Roach inside the factory building.

Turk put out a big hand to push him aside, confident he had nothing to fear while Kenny covered him. Diamond grabbed hold of his arm and jerked him forward, off balance, and turned him around. He held Turk tightly in front of his body, using him as a shield, staring into the muzzle of Kenny's gun.

Kenny snapped off a shot that missed by a hair's breadth and ricochetted off the doorframe into the factory. Turk screamed, 'Don't shoot, Kenny — for Christ's sake, don't shoot!'

Diamond held Turk in a stranglehold, watching Kenny creep forward and sideways, looking for a clear shot at him. He waited till the lanky gunman got to within a few yards, then braced himself and catapulted Turk forward with every ounce of muscle he possessed.

Kenny tried to dodge but was far too slow. Turk cannoned into him, knocking the gun from his hand. Kenny went down on his back, swearing, with Turk's heavy body sprawled on top of him.

Diamond stepped forward, drawing his revolver.

Kenny wriggled out from under the big enforcer, his hand darting along the ground, groping for his gun.

'Leave it!'

Kenny looked up at Diamond's face and stopped trying. His expression contorted with viciousness, and Diamond didn't doubt that if he'd had his gun he would use it with intent to kill.

Turk rose unsteadily, reeling like a drunk, half-stunned.

'Now get going,' Diamond said, revolver steady in his hand. 'And forget about coming back.'

Kenny scrambled to his feet. 'Mr. Greco will nail you for this, spade. You've really got it coming to you.'

'Move out!'

Kenny and Turk turned away and walked towards their car. Diamond stepped inside the doorway, watching them closely. The car took off in a hurry with Kenny handling it like a racing driver, changing down and accelerating. It hurtled through the open gate out of the yard.

Diamond waited, listening to the sound of the engine fade away, then he scooped up Kenny's gun and went inside, calling: 'Roach? All clear — they've left.'

His voice echoed hollowly in the barn of a factory. There was no answer. Maybe Roach had got scared and skipped out the back way. Diamond walked down the aisle between plastic-topped benches, noting absently that things looked different; some pieces of equipment had gone.

He called again and still there was no answer except the echo of his own voice, and no sign of Roach. Then he heard an engine start up beyond the loading bay and quickened his step.

He reached the rear loading door, half-open in its slide-grooves, in time to see a van accelerate away. As it turned, he caught a glimpse of the driver in the light of the moon; he was almost sure it was Roach.

The van was a plain one and its rear

number plate was obscured by mud.

Diamond retraced his way through the factory, looking at the workbenches with a keen eye. Exactly what was different? He saw that Roach hadn't bothered with any of the copies, but the master tapes and all the video machines were gone.

He laughed aloud in the empty shed and the sound echoed. Greco was due for an unpleasant surprise when he learnt that Roach had skipped with his equipment. The Fox had been out-foxed this time.

Diamond left by the front gate, whistling *Tiger Rag*, and started to walk back to his office and bed.

★   ★   ★

Detective Cave pushed back his Panana hat and lit a cigarette as he perched on one corner of Diamond's desk. Morning sunlight came through the open window and illuminating his face so that the wrinkles looked as though they had been etched in black ink.

He listened, smiling as Diamond

related the events of the previous evening, his gaze not moving from the private investigator's chocolate face. When Diamond finished he burst out laughing.

'That's the only laugh I've had in a long time. Yeah, I like it. Greco pays Roach, who pays you — with Greco's own money — to protect him from Greco. You get the jump on his gunsel and enforcer and send 'em crawling home. Then Roach scoots off with the Fox's porno set-up, to start an operation of his own someplace. But not in New Orleans, that's all I care about. Well, every little helps in the fight against organised crime. You reckon we should team up as a double act?'

His harsh laughter turned into a fit of coughing and he stubbed out his cigarette and tossed the butt through the open window.

Diamond opened his desk drawer and took out a gun, holding it by the barrel as he handed it to the detective. 'Kenny dropped this.'

'I just bet he did.'

Cave removed the cartridges and

slipped the gun into his pocket. 'I'll take charge of it.' Still smiling, he adjusted his Panama. 'Watch yourself, pal — Greco could be hopping mad.'

He paused in the doorway.

'I'll have to see if I can't push another client your way.'

Then his shoes clattered down the stairs.

8

Snake Dancer

The grey Ford edged forward a few yards, stopped, edged forward again, creeping through the mid-day traffic. Kenny babbled lasciviously to himself at the wheel.

Leon Greco, immaculate in a grey suit recently dry-cleaned, sat in the back and looked out at the cars jamming Royal Street. New Orleans was a convention center and that suited him very well at the moment.

The Ford stopped again and Greco became aware that Kenny was watching him in the rearview mirror. The gunman's face looked as sharp as a hatchet, his lips tight — pressed into a vicious line. He knew what the trouble was: Kenny had lost one of his precious guns.

'You ought to let me kill Diamond.'

'No.' Greco raised his voice, almost

explosively. 'Leave him alone — that's an order. What is he, after all? A two-bit private eye. I should waste my time on such garbage.'

He remembered the phone call from the factory that morning: Roach had skipped, taking the videos and masters with him. It was a fleabite, nothing. Roach would have had more sense than to stay in Louisiana. Well, good riddance to bad rubbish.

'You drive the car, Kenny, and protect me and that's all. If I want a hit done, I'll bring in somebody from out of town.'

Kenny didn't reply immediately, concentrating on pushing the Ford forward a few more yards. When they stopped, he said sullenly, 'Then let Turk have him. He's sore too.'

'Maybe I should hire Wash back? He takes your gun away and beats up Turk — what are you, a couple of amateurs?' Greco made a small sigh. 'Anyway, I'll need Turk for another job soon.'

The car gained some more yards and braked.

'I just don't know what's got into you,

Mr. Greco,' Kenny said finally. 'You've changed. You don't seem to care that Roach ripped you off, or anything else these days.'

And that's the truth, Greco thought, and smiled. He had more important things on his mind, like the contacts he was making to get Madden's team together. Like his future. He wasn't interested in the rackets any more. He was just going through the motions and waiting . . .

★ ★ ★

Diamond and Chelsea had lunch together in a small restaurant in the French Quarter, platters of bar-b-que ribs in sauce with bread and whipped butter followed by ice cream. He was in a good mood and, as they made their way back through Jackson Square, past the artists showing their work, he thought it would be nice to have a portrait of Chelsea for his temporary home.

He paused looking at some of the

sketches on view, hung on iron railings.

'A quick sketch sir? Only takes ten minutes.'

The artist was a wizened little man wearing smock and beret.

'Yeah,' Diamond said. 'My girlfriend. Charcoal.'

'If you'll sit here, Miss?'

Chelsea was startled. 'What is this, Wash?'

He grinned. 'Just a notion I have. Maybe one day you'll be famous . . . and my sketch will be worth something.'

Chelsea put out her tongue, but sat down. No one had ever wanted a portrait of her before and she had a warm feeling for Wash for thinking of it.

Diamond watched the artist limn in her features with a few sure strokes of charcoal. She seemed to come alive on the buff paper; the sun catching her love of life, the dazzling smile, her dark beauty.

'That's great, man!'

'My pleasure, sir,' the artist said as Diamond paid him.

Then they walked slowly back to the office through narrow streets, beneath the iron-grille balconies of old houses. The muggy air smelt strongly of magnolia blossom.

They reached the Coin-op shop and climbed the stairs to find a client waiting. Middle-aged and dapper, he perched on the edge of the visitor's chair, hands clasped over a silver-topped cane. He wore a white suit, longish grey hair brushed straight back and a worried expression.

Diamond slid into his swivel seat behind the desk while Chelsea went into the back room and closed the door.

'What can I do for you?'

This client was white and obviously a tourist; judging by the quality of his suit, a man with money and something of an aristocratic air.

'My name is Leland and I want you to find my daughter.' He produced a colour photograph from his pocket and passed it across the desk.

Diamond saw a studio portrait of a young girl with fair hair and freckles. He decided she had the pugnacious look of a natural rebel.

Leland confirmed his impression with his next words. 'Ella has always been something of a problem — now she's just plain wild. She dropped out of college, and that's a pity because she's bright.'

He tapped at the floor with his cane as if he regretted not using it on his daughter when she was younger.

'She's running with a wild bunch and is into sex and drugs, rock music, hot-rods and demonstrations and everything else going. Everything except work, that is. Now, apparently, it's voodoo. She's caught up in some religious cult and I'm scared for her.'

For a moment, Leland looked uncertain. 'You're not a believer, Mr. Diamond? No offense was intended, I assure you.'

Diamond smiled easily. 'And none taken, Mr. Leland. You mustn't think that everyone descended from African blood worships the voodoo gods.'

'I want Ella back.'

'How old is she?'

'Twenty-one — just.'

'I can try.' Diamond said. 'I don't

doubt I can track her down, but as an adult, she'll have a mind of her own. I can't force her to return if she doesn't want to.'

Leland nodded. 'Possibly you can show her the error in her reasoning — or lack of it. If you can show her this cult is phony. I believe she'll get the message quick enough.'

'Do you happen to know where this cult meets, or who runs it?'

'The leader calls himself Doctor Ambrose — that's all I've been able to find out and why I've come to you. I assume you have contacts.'

Diamond nodded. 'I charge a hundred a day and expenses for as long as I work on the job.'

'Agreed.' Leland rose to his feet and limped to the door, bearing down on his cane. 'I shall hope to see Ella shortly.'

As he clumped down the stairs, the door of the back room opened and Chelsea came through. Her normally sunny face was disturbed.

'You shouldn't mix in witch things, Wash.'

Diamond laughed. 'Don't tell me you believe this voodoo crap? You can bet your last dollar it's a trap for the tourists. They fall for it and Ambrose makes money the easy way.'

'Perhaps.' Chelsea moved uneasily about the office. 'I don't like it, that's all. You stick your nose into voodoo, and all sorts of unpleasant things happen. I had an aunt who was a witch.' She shivered at a childhood memory.

'So, what happened?'

'My Aunt Rebecca, when I was young and living in the back country — another woman tried to take her man away. She made a sacrifice at sunset and said the words. Then she dreamed of the other woman, dreamed of a poisonous snake biting her and her whole body swelling up. Next day she was told that the woman died of snake bite in the night. Just suppose Ambrose isn't a phony?'

'All the more reason to get the girl away from him. Have you ever heard of this Ambrose?'

'I haven't heard anything good about

him. He has a temple across the river, in Algiers — off Pelican Avenue some-where.'

Diamond slipped into his jacket. 'I'll just snoop around a little.'

'Be careful, Wash.'

'Sure, baby.'

Diamond drove his Mustang onto the bridge over the Mississippi and into the suburbs on the west bank. Pelican Avenue was easy enough to find and he coasted through a residential area, quiet in daytime, till he found a gas station, and asked.

'Doc Ambrose? Sure thing . . . four blocks along and turn left.'

He located the temple and parked opposite. It was one of the older buildings, a small hall that had been allowed to run down. Probably Ambrose got it cheap, and hadn't even bothered to tart it up to catch the suckers.

He crossed the road and tried the door, it was locked, and a notice read:

CHURCH OF DAMBALLA
Evening Service 8.30

Diamond looked at his watch and drove on till he found a coffee bar and passed the waiting time with the local paper. As it grew dark, he drove back to the church hall and parked in the shadow of a tree across the street, and watched the entrance.

He saw late workers speeding home and presently the dim street lights came on; it was too hot to leave the windows closed and he sat breathing gasoline fumes.

Then cars began to arrive at the hall, lights appeared at the windows and the front door opened. Diamond waited, watching the tourists flock to be fleeced. A crowd gathered around the porch, talking desultorily. A bunch of young dropouts drifted up and he took a keen look at one; a slim boyish figure, hip-hugging Levis and tank top, fair hair. He thought he recognized Ella Leland.

Inside, a drummer started up and the night throbbed with sound, a monotonous slow beat, calling the faithful to the service.

Diamond left his Mustang and crossed

over to be met at the door by a young man with a collection box. He folded a dollar bill and pushed it through the slot and walked inside.

The sultry atmosphere seemed worse in the fiery red lighting with a drummer, cross-legged in shadow, pursuing his unvarying beat. People stood around, close to the walls, chatting in low voices. There was an altar with black candles. The single drumbeat went on and on, a dull rhythm destroying his capacity to think clearly.

Diamond began to angle towards the group of youngsters with Ella Leland when a curtain parted behind the altar and a man stepped through. Diamond froze. The drumbeat changed, quickened to work up to a crescendo, and stooped.

In the silence, Doctor Ambrose smiled and raised one brown hand. He spoke in a quiet penetrating voice that reached to every corner of the hall.

'My friends — '

The drummer struck a single beat.

'Welcome to the Temple of Damballa — '

The drum beat once.

'To my regular parishioners I say, worship in peace — '

Another single beat.

'To those of you who appear for the first time — '

One drumbeat.

'Welcome, and I hope you will enjoy our simple service.'

The drum rolled like muted thunder in the distance.

Diamond studied Ambrose. His skin was light brown, his hair a dusty grey and his voice held a hypnotic quality. He wore a dark suit and gold-rimmed spectacles and when the light caught the lenses, his eyes seemed blank and staring.

A black hand holding a live chicken came through the curtain and passed it to Doctor Ambrose. Doctor of what? Diamond wondered. With a deft movement, Ambrose cut the bird with a small knife so that blood ran into a silver cup resting on the altar.

'Damballa, we offer this sacrifice in Thy name.'

He brought the cup to his lips, sipped,

and passed it to a member of the congregation. Each person sipped the hot blood and passed on the cup. Visitors passed it on quickly without tasting.

When the empty cup returned to Ambrose, he placed it on the altar and lifted his face, smiling. It was the smile of a shark scenting a shoal of small fish.

'I call on Damballa the snake god of ancient Africa.' The drum beat once. 'Now he will reveal his Power.'

The drapes parted again and a black man carried in a wicker basket and placed it before the altar. Doctor Ambrose moved to one side as two more drummers took their place, sitting cross-legged on the floor. The drummers pounded out a dance rhythm until the walls of the hall began to shake.

Diamond found his own feet tapping. His glance moved over the white visitors, sure now that the girl he'd seen earlier was Ella Leland. Her freckled face glowed with excitement.

A dancer swept through the curtains into the hall; she was young and lithe and naked to the waist. She had olive-tinted skin and wide dark eyes and dark hair, cut short. Pointed breasts jutted and she wore only a G-string under a transparent ankle-length skirt slit to her thigh.

She threw back the lid of the wicker basket, caught up a python and began dancing, slowly at first, encouraging the snake to slither over her shoulders and around her hips.

The drums quickened their beating as she glided around the hall and there was no other sound. The audience held its breath, listening to the drums and watching the girl.

Again the drumbeat quickened and the dancer worked herself into a frenzy, bare breasts shaking, juggling the big snake in her hands to prevent its coils tightening about her neck. The quick violent beat was hypnotic. Faster and faster she whirled on powerful dancer's legs, sweat trickling down her body, hips undulating and skirt flaring. The drums pounded louder and louder.

The congregation began to chant and clap and stamp, echoing the beat, swaying in unison with the dancer and the sinuous body of the python. She achieved ecstasy.

Diamond found himself held by her performance; he knew what was happening to him, what was happening to everyone in the hall. He found himself believing; the atmosphere was getting to him. His blood was roused and his pulse reverberated to the incessant rhythm of the drums. He was becoming mesmerised.

One thing was certain; Doctor Ambrose knew how to stage a performance.

Fighting to retain a hold on his reason, Diamond began slowly to edge a way through the foot-stamping, hand-clapping crowd to the door. Once outside, he used his handkerchief to mop the sweat from his face and crossed the street to his car. He slid behind the wheel, closed the windows and turned the radio dial till he found music to combat the insidious drumming from the hall. He tuned to a Mozart quartet and settled to wait for the show to end.

The drumming seemed to go on for hours, louder and faster, to reach a dramatic climax — and then stop abruptly. It was as if a storm ended in the middle of a roll of thunder. Total silence blanketed the suburb and Diamond wondered if he'd been struck deaf. Then, gradually, normal night sounds — a car horn, the clip-clop of stiletto heels on the sidewalk, a distant shout — filtered in over the Mozart.

People began to leave the temple, putting money in the collection box in the porch. Diamond was willing to bet that box pulled in a lot of dough at each performance.

He switched off his radio and got out of the car, watching for Ella Leland. He saw her come out with a bunch of teenagers; she looked excited and some of the group appeared to be in a daze, as if the drumming had been too much to take.

Diamond moved fast to cut her out from the group. 'Miss Leland?'

'Yes . . . what is it?'

'Quite a show that,' he said casually. 'Phony as hell, of course. That Ambrose character must be really raking in the dough.' He laughed, including her in the put-down.

Ella Leland stared coldly at him. 'Some people believe it to be a genuine religious experience, Mr. — ?'

'Diamond's the name. Now, Miss Leland, you're an intelligent person so you don't have to fall for any old flimflam. You and I both know — '

She cut in sharply. 'Did my father put you up to this?'

'He's concerned for you, yes.'

'Well, I'm free, white and twenty-one and I've just found what I've been looking for all my life. I'm not going back, Mr. Diamond, and you can tell my father that.'

She turned abruptly and hurried after her friends, leaving Diamond a rear view of her Levis and credit cards sticking up from a pocket. She didn't look round and he got in his Mustang and started the engine. He waited for the group to get some way ahead and then followed, driving slowly and hanging back.

Ella Leland and her friends turned

into Vallette Street and entered a dilapidated house not far from the river. Diamond cruised past, made a mental note of the number and went home.

9

Target for Tonight

Fred Cave sat alone at a table outside a waterfront bar near the Moon Walk, sipping ice-cold beer and staring gloomily at a dull red sunset over the Mississipi. The other tables were crowded with tourists, but nobody joined him; maybe it was his sour expression or maybe they smelt cop. In any case, it was too hot to worry about.

He was officially off-duty and feeling depressed. Most other detectives would have been glad of a few hours freedom, but Cave couldn't face going home to an empty house. He used the place to sleep, take a shower and change his shirt. How long was it since Mae had left? Damn near eighteen months, he calculated. How long since he'd had a proper meal? Or gone to a concert? Or had a woman stay the night?

Everything seemed too much bother. He lived now only for his work; it had been like that before, he admitted, and that was why Mae left him. It was the reason a lot of cops' wives split; they couldn't stand the long hours and uncertainty.

He got depressed just thinking about the germs; the pushers and muggers, rape-artists and thieves and conmen.

And the corruption. The force was just another bureaucracy nowadays — full of young career types busy keeping their noses clean, pushing for promotion and sitting on their asses waiting for the pension to arrive. Time-servers. Cave despised them. That wasn't police work.

A shadow passed across his face and Breeze dropped into the seat opposite. Cave bought two beers.

The informer sat in shadow, floppy hair hiding his face. 'I hear the word's gone out for Earl Vogel.'

Cave's lip curled back. Another scumbag.

'You know where he hangs out?'

'Of course I know,' Cave snapped. 'A

pusher, strictly small-time. It'll be Turk, I suppose?'

'I suppose.'

'Yeah, well, thanks. I'll have a think what to do about it — if anything.'

Breeze drained the last of his beer and slid away into the night, as silent as any ghost.

Cave lit a Marlboro and listened absently to the tourist talk around him. Sin City, they called it. You could buy anything — openly — in New Orleans.

And filth like Greco got rich on it. Cave considered how he might use this bit of information. He didn't give a shit what happened to Earl Vogel, but there had to be an angle he could use, somewhere. Tip off Diamond? He could still raise a smile when he remembered how Roach had ripped off the Fox. Maybe . . .

★   ★   ★

Kenny's room was small, the walls covered with full-size colour posters of glamour models. On the bedside table were stacked piles of girlie magazines.

The door of the room was locked.

Kenny unlocked the wall cupboard and got out his guns, handling them with the loving care another might give his woman. He broke down each one, cleaned and oiled and checked the mechanism, reassembled them. His collection was his joy and pride.

He hefted each one in his hand. A Luger. A .45 revolver. A small automatic. Finally he decided on the .38 Colt with a short barrel, grieving over the loss of its mate.

It would be nice to use it on Diamond, but Mr. Greco had said 'no', and he was the boss. Kenny didn't understand what Greco was up to these days but he wasn't going to disobey, not all the time he paid big money.

He slid the gun into his shoulder holster and put on his jacket, slipped a couple of boxes of shells in his pocket. He locked the rest of his armoury in the cupboard and turned to study the posters on the wall.

'Which one? Blonde, brunette, red-head? Nude or sexy lingerie? He thought of Diamond and his brown-skinned girlfriend and laughed as he took down a picture of a young negress. 'Yeah, just the job . . . '

He rolled the poster and tucked it under his arm, picked up a box of brass thumb-tacks. He went out, locking the door after him. Whistling, he walked along the street to a gun club he used and down the steps to the underground target range.

This early in the evening, there weren't many using the range. Just a couple of kids, barely out of their teens; amateurs, Kenny thought disparagingly. The air echoed to gunshots and smelt of cordite fumes; it was a sound and smell he enjoyed.

The floor was sand and there was a rack of fire extinguishers at the bottom of the stairs. Never been checked in years, he thought; probably they'd never work if there was a fire.

He shucked his coat and loosened the revolver in its holster. Target for tonight, he reflected happily, and pinned up his poster; a dark-skinned model, wearing high heels and stockings supported by a frilly white suspender-belt, tiny briefs and a half-cup bra.

He licked his lips as he drew his gun and took aim at her right breast. 'Bitch!' he hissed, and emptied his .38, obliterating the bra cup.

He reloaded, drew himself up to his full height and aimed at the left cup. 'Black whore!' He fired all chambers, destroying her bra.

Again he reloaded. 'Cow!' He wiped out her briefs.

Kenny stared at the cutout figure, naked except for stockings and suspender-belt and shoes. He felt good, all tension drained out of him. He reloaded and holstered his gun.

When he left the range, he was clear-headed, all thought of Diamond gone from his mind.

★   ★   ★

The ground floor bar at the *Hotel de Paris* was a madhouse. Leon Greco sat in an alcove off the main lounge, drawing on a Cuban cigar and smiling with satisfaction. In front of him was a low table with a tray of bottles and glasses and a plastic sign lettered:

PRIVATE

The lounge was crammed with salesmen. The *Paris* was entertaining a sales convention and it sounded like feeding time at the zoo. The monkey house, Greco thought. Each salesman appeared to be trying to drink his rival under the table and flog him Brooklyn Bridge at the same time. It made good cover for a meeting.

Every now and again, he had to insist that his alcove was booked for a private meeting. Most of the conventioneers were well-oiled and unsteady on their feet and into dirty jokes. Greco had had no difficulty in borrowing a name badge from someone who'd passed out early. Nobody would be able to overhear what was discussed and, if each interview went briskly, he'd be in and out of the hotel before the management realised he wasn't with the convention at all.

He sat smoking and smiling, totally relaxed and wearing his borrowed badge: *Al Bonney Detroit*.

The first man pushed through the crowd and dropped into the seat next to Greco.

'A drink?'

'Straight bourbon.'

Greco poured and Blackie Hendriks tossed it down in a single gulp. He had a bruiser's face and a reputation for armed robbery. He wore a business suit that was tight under the arms and wiped sweat from his face with a tissue.

'Some crush, huh?'

Greco leaned close so they could hear each other above the noise. 'I'm hiring for Madden. Are you interested?'

'Madden? Sure.'

'It's a team job — a job for people who don't lose their cool. No guns allowed.'

'That's okay if it's Madden. What he says goes.'

'Good.' Greco had the feeling this was going to be a cinch. 'I may be hiring for other organisers in the future. D'you want me to put your name on my books for regular work?'

'Sure, why not?'

Greco nodded, pleased. 'Right, I'll be in touch.'

As Blackie rose and disappeared into the convention crowd, Greco glanced at his watch. He'd set the intervals at fifteen minutes; he had a couple of minutes in hand. He lit a fresh cigar while he waited for the second man.

Ted Paley was slim and wiry and known as a hot get-away driver. He, too was impressed by Madden's name and readily agreed to take the job. He said he didn't drink and looked as cold as a chip off an iceberg.

Greco had refused even to consider Kenny for the team; he didn't want Kenny or anyone else to know what he was doing. He wanted the new life he was building in a separate compartment. As for Turk, he had Vogel to take care of.

Two more strong-arms and another driver and he had it wrapped up. Each time he emphasised that this was only the first job, hinting that he had more work lined up for them.

At the end of the interviews, he felt satisfied he'd made a start in his new career — one that wouldn't leave him exposed to any risk at all.

He discarded his borrowed convention badge, and slipped the PRIVATE notice into his pocket and lavishly tipped the waiter who'd kept his table supplied. Leon Greco edged through the noisy crowd in the foyer, out into the quiet of Royal Street.

★   ★   ★

'I'm not getting mixed up with Doc Ambrose,' Chelsea stated resolutely. 'No way am I getting into voodoo.'

Diamond sighed and glanced at the charcoal portrait on the wall of his office; the artist seemed to have missed out the stubborn part of her character.

'I'm not asking you to,' he said patiently. He'd filled her in on his trip to Algiers and his meeting with Ella Leland. 'I just thought you might know the dancer Ambrose uses. I got the impression she was a professional show dancer, is all.'

Morning sunlight slanted through the open window and turned his Hawaiian shirt to a tapestry of many colours as they sat drinking coffee.

'I only ever heard of one dancer who does a sort of voodoo act. Her name's Julie something or other, and she works in cabaret. I've no idea where she might be — '

Above the clatter of washing machines below, they heard quiet footsteps on the stairs. Chelsea got up from the client's chair.

'See you later, Wash. I'll try to get a line on Julie for you. Somebody at the club might know where she hangs out.'

As she went through the doorway, a man came in. He was lean and unshaven with long greasy hair. Diamond had the feeling he'd seen him somewhere before, but couldn't place him.

His visitor wore a linen jacket that needed cleaning, patched jeans and pointed shoes with badly scuffed heels.

He smelt of back alleys and garbage.

He stood looking around the office, nodded to Diamond and slid into a chair. He had a smile like a snarl.

'Heard tell you're standing up to Greco,' he drawled. 'And I need somebody on my side against his new thug. How's about it?'

Diamond placed him. Earl Vogel, a small-tine drug pusher, one of a chain that Greco supplied.

'Are you trying to take over?' he asked bluntly.

Vogel gave a casual shrug. 'So what if I am? I can pay you. Greco's losing his grip — lots of the boys are figuring it's time to break away and set up on their own. I just want someone between me and Turk.'

Diamond got himself a glass of water from the cooler and thought about it. He despised the dope business and felt only loathing for the man seated across from his desk. He'd seen too many lives ruined, kids dragged down to gutter level — but this was another chance to get back at Greco. He could do something about Vogel afterwards.

'Okay,' he said. 'I'll keep Turk off your back for a century a day.'

'That's great, man.' Vogel pulled a wad of notes from his back pocket and peeled off one hundred dollars. 'I'll pay cash each day, okay?'

Diamond nodded, strapped on his shoulder holster and went down the stairs with his new client.

'Reckon there'll be nothing happening till tonight,' Vogel drawled as they hit the street. 'We'll go back to my place. I have to hang around there for a phone call — I'm waiting on a supply coming in.'

They walked along Chartres and cut through the French Market, piled high with fruit and vegetables. Vogel lived in and operated his business from one room in a drab hotel: it was a top floor room, with a fire escape climbing down the rear wall.

Diamond checked that door and window were locked. There was no air-conditioning and the air was like treacle.

Vogel was amused. 'They ain't going to come here — they'll try to hit me after dark when I'm doing my rounds. You can bet on it.'

'It's your life you're betting on.'

The telephone rang and Vogel grabbed it. 'Yeah . . . tonight, okay . . . the usual place.' He cut off quickly. 'Let's grab something to eat while we can.'

They went out to a diner around the corner for chicken and French fries and apple strudel. Diamond bought two cans of Pepsi to take back with him.

Upstairs again, Earl Vogel sprawled out on the bed and cat-napped. Diamond took a hard chair, jacket off, by the window, his nose wrinkling at the smell. A professional couldn't always pick his jobs, and stay in business.

A tap dripped. A cockroach scuttled across the floor. Diamond relaxed, waiting for darkness.

He sipped Pepsi and watched the river from the window. The dockside was busy, ships loading and unloading, whores picking up sailors; a group of tourists boarded a replica paddle-steamer. He watched, and listened.

Gradually twilight came and shadows gathered.

10

Alley Corpse

Earl Vogel awoke. He rolled off his bed, went to a sink in the corner of the room and splashed water on his face. He dried his hands on a dirty towel.

'Time to go,' he drawled. 'This is where you start earning your money.'

Diamond stood up and slipped on his jacket, checked that his revolver was ready to hand and preceded the drug pusher down the stairs. A bare bulb glowed in the stairwell and there was garbage littering the hallway. He looked both ways outside; there were the usual crowds on the sidewalk but nobody acting suspiciously. Vogel took the lead, turning confidently into an unlit alley alongside the hotel.

They were halfway through the alley when a big figure loomed out of shadow and hands closed around Vogel's throat.

Diamond recognised Turk and moved

fast; he gripped Turk's little fingers and bent them back to break his hold. He slammed Greco's new enforcer hard against the wall and Vogel jumped clear.

Turk's small eyes gleamed in folds of flesh. 'You again! This time, Diamond, I'm going to — '

Diamond ducked as Turk swung a ham-sized fist, grabbed his arm and smashed him against the wall again.

Vogel's voice betrayed excitement as he shouted encouragement. 'That's the stuff, Wash — give it to him!'

But the ex-wrestler was big and strong and knew all the dirty tricks; he wasn't someone to fool around with in a dark alley. Diamond wanted the fight over quickly.

Turk lashed out at his knee-cap and Diamond backed away, luring him off-balance; then he went in under the powerful arms reaching for him, gripped Turk's nose with the fingers of one hand and forced his head back.

Turk squealed, and Diamond chopped at the exposed throat with the side of his free hand, held flat and rigid as a board, hurting his damaged voice-box.

Turk gave a high-pitched whining sound and sank down against the wall, hands going to his throat as he gasped for air. He sat in smelly garbage, wheezing like a leaky balloon.

Vogel darted forward eagerly, ready to use his pointed shoes.

Diamond looked past him and glimpsed a moving shadow. 'Get down!'

There was a sharp crack, a stabbing tongue of flame and Vogel shuddered and crashed to the ground.

Diamond dived flat, drawing his revolver and cursing. He heard soft running footfalls and crawled towards Vogel's body. The bullet had smashed into his back at close range, penetrating the heart and exited through his chest; blood pumped like an obscene fountain and Diamond had seen enough gunshot wounds to know he was beyond help.

He moved warily down the alley. It was dark, silent. There came a metallic clatter as his foot kicked something; the killer had discarded his revolver and fled. Diamond didn't touch it. He continued to the end of the alley, but there was no sign of the gunman.

He puzzled over it. If Greco had sent Turk to punish Vogel, then who had shot him? And why?

Diamond walked back to the corpse. Turk had dragged himself away, obviously reluctant to be involved.

Diamond returned to the hotel and used their telephone to call the police, then waited beside the body.

He did not have long to wait before he heard the wail of a siren. A white Ford cruiser arrived with dome-light flashing and a squeal of brakes. Two uniformed patrolmen jumped out.

'Hold it right there, boy!'

The first cop held a gun pointed at him.

'Now face the wall, arms out, lean against it. Legs apart — up on your toes!'

Diamond obeyed. The second patrolman made a body search, took his revolver and sniffed the barrel.

'This hasn't been fired.'

'Who're you, black boy? Turn around and answer me — how come you're carrying a piece? You got a license?'

Diamond turned slowly. 'Can I get my wallet out?'

'Sure you can — nice and easy unless you want a hole in yuh.'

Diamond pulled out his wallet, opened it to show his I.D.

'Private snooper, huh?' The patrolman didn't seem impressed.

His partner crouched beside the body of Earl Vogel. 'This one's a goner — better call for the meat wagon.'

'The gun's in the alley,' Diamond said.

'We'll do the police work — you just answer questions. What do you know about the dead man?'

By the time Diamond had told his story, an unmarked car arrived with a couple of plainclothes men. One, burly with brown eyes and unruly hair, introduced himself as Detective Jessel. He took Diamond through his story again after personally checking his I.D.

'He could have had two guns,' his partner said, 'and planted the one he used in the alley.'

'You-all know why I should kill my own

128

client?' Diamond protested.

'You tell us.'

Jessel came to a decision. 'You carry on here, Mac. The lieutenant will want to question this witness — I'll take him in now.'

Diamond got in the police car and Jessel drove to the station, parked and they went upstairs to the squadroom. There was a harsh light from overhead fluorescent tubes and a green glow from banks of VDUs; the smell of stale cigarette smoke and a clatter from typing. Someone swore into a telephone.

They walked past a bulletin board and threaded a way between desks on the way to an office at the rear. Cave, feet up on his desk, winked as Diamond went by.

Jessel knocked lightly on a frosted glass door that had painted on it: *Lieutenant of Detectives*.

An unhurried voice called, 'Come in.'

Jessel opened the door and motioned Diamond through. The office was small and square with one window covered by a grille, cupboard and hat stand, a desk with a plastic nameplate:

Detective Lieutenant Stoner

While Jessel gave him a quick run-down on the murder, Diamond studied Cave's superior officer. Stoner had greying hair and rimless spectacles; his dress was neat and his manner appeared mild — but the mildness might prove deceptive.

Stoner took Diamond through his story for a third time, asking questions, and checked his I.D. yet again. His face grew suspicious, his voice hard.

'You're known, Diamond. You don't have a record, but we know you worked for Greco as an enforcer. So just how did you come by an investigator's license?'

'Well, now, your Detective Cave arranged that.'

Stoner's eyebrows lifted. 'Did he now?' he said softly, and then raised his voice. 'Fred, move your ass in here.'

When Cave arrived, he was preceded by a second man wearing denim and long greasy hair.

'Phillips, narcotics,' he said, flashing a badge. 'About your murder victim, Earl Vogel, a pusher. We've had an eye on him

130

for a while. Small-time, we were hoping for a lead to his supplier. That's cooked, of course. Apart from that, he's no loss to anybody.'

Stoner's back stiffened as if someone had stuck a stair rod down it. 'It's still murder, and it's my job to investigate.'

Phillips shrugged as if he couldn't have cared less.

Diamond volunteered, 'Vogel was only a link in a chain — at least, that's what he told me.'

'You did a great job of protecting him,' Stoner said coldly, and turned his gaze on Cave. 'Suppose you explain why you got a P.I. license for Greco's enforcer?'

Cave lit a Marlboro and spoke casually. 'Diamond's okay — I checked him out. He'd already quit Greco, and the Fox sent someone round — probably Turk — to wreck his apartment. He's legit now.'

Stoner glared at his detective with compressed lips, then turned to Jessel.

'Type up Diamond's statement and get him to sign it. You can give him back his gun. And you, black boy, keep your nose clean or I'll have your license. You hear me? Fred, stay behind — I want to talk to you.'

After Jessel, Diamond and Phillips had left the office, Stoner said quietly: 'Close the door.'

Cave obeyed and took a seat, tapping ash into the desk tray.

'You set this up, Fred. Just what the hell are you playing at?'

'Diamond was protecting his client.'

'The police give any protection necessary. You know that.'

'To a drug pedlar?'

Lieutenant Harry Stoner didn't answer. He loosened his tie as though he were strangling.

Cave's face bore the hint of a sneer as he asked, 'Are you really worried about one less pusher?'

'You're playing a dangerous game, Fred. If you're caught out, there'll be nothing I can do for you. Now bring in Turk for questioning.'

Cave stubbed out his cigarette and rose to his feet.

'I don't like to see the germs get away

with it all the time . . . you might try tying the murder weapon to Kenny.' His lips curved in a bitter smile. 'And I bet you five Greco's lawyer will spring him before you even get to question him.'

* * *

Leon Greco looked up from behind his desk in his import-export office. He wore a harassed expression and artificial light put dark shadows under his eyes. He looked as if he couldn't believe what Turk had just told him.

The enforcer's face was pale as chalk and he continually massaged his throat with his fingers. He had difficulty talking and it had taken a while to get the full story out of him.

'What the hell's going on?' Greco demanded. 'I didn't order Earl shot — who could have done it? Do you know anything about this, Kenny?'

'Not me,' the lanky gunman said uneasily. 'You sure it wasn't Wash, Turk?'

'I'm — sure,' Turk croaked.

'Then it must be someone trying to

muscle in on the dope business.'

'You'd better have a damn good alibi if you want my lawyer to represent you.'

'I was with you,' Kenny said. 'Remember?'

His gaze rested on the wall behind Greco's head, where a glamour calendar showed a redhead in fishnet stockings. His tongue moistened his lips.

'Yeah, I remember.' Greco sighed. He hadn't slept well the previous night and his stomach was upset.

As if he didn't have enough trouble with double-crossing managers and the cops starting to put pressure on . . . now this stupid murder, trying to tie Kenny in. He worried that it might interfere with his new set-up.

He reached in his jacket for his wallet, and extracted several large bills. 'Turk, you'd better lie low for a few days. Take a trip somewhere.'

'Right, Mr. Greco.'

Leon Greco rose from his desk and switched off the light. He locked the office and got into his grey Ford. Kenny drove.

After a pause, Greco said. 'What does Wash think he's doing? This is the second time he's interfered.'

'Looks like he's got it in for you personally.'

'Stupid, stupid.' Greco shook his head sadly, then lit a cigar. 'I'll have to fix that son-of-a-bitch. I'll fix him real good.'

11

The Fix

Diamond and Chelsea sprawled happy but exhausted in a rumpled bed. It was almost three o'clock in the morning, after a session at the *Black Cat*, and Chelsea had insisted on his coming back to her place because, as she put it, 'My bed's bigger than yours.'

She curled up inside his arms and was dozing off when she remembered. It had gone right out of her head when she heard he'd been mixed up in a shooting and had been taken to police headquarters. All she could think of then was that he might have been killed.

'Voodoo dancer,' she mumbled into his armpit.

'What was that, baby?'

'Julie — the dancer you asked after. Besides working for Doc Ambrose, she does an act at the *Folies Club*.'

136

'That's great,' Diamond said sleepily. 'Guess I'll look her up tomorrow.'

★ ★ ★

By daylight, the *Folies* off Bourbon didn't look anything special. The frontage was narrow, the doorway set back and the photographs of topless dancers seemed strangely old-fashioned. There were no bright lights, no music and no customers.

Diamond kept hammering on the door until someone opened it; a shrivelled-up man with a broom nearly as tall as himself. Behind him, Diamond caught sight of chairs piled on tables in dim lighting.

'Yes, what is it now?'

'I'm trying to locate Julie.'

'She isn't here and, anyway, she ain't that sort.'

'This is business. I just need her address, and she'll thank you for giving it.'

The cleaner sniffed and wiped his nose on his sleeve. Diamond folded a twenty and passed it to a gnarled hand.

'That's different. She's got a place on Lafayette, near the old City Hall — the Pyramid — but she sure ain't going to like you for getting her out of bed before midday.'

Diamond drove west along Bourbon, crossed Canal and continued through the business section till he reached Lafayette Street. He located the Pyramid, a new tower block that rose in concrete and glass steps, glanced at his watch and looked for a parking slot. He found a café and lingered over a couple of cups of coffee.

It was just noon when he walked into the foyer and asked for her apartment number, took the elevator and leaned on the bell-push.

The door opened a fraction and Julie brushed back tousled hair from her eyes. 'I don't know you.'

Diamond showed his P.I. license and said, 'I need your help, Miss, and I'm willing to pay you.'

'Yeah? Well, come on in — all I ever seem to meet is men who want something for nothing.'

The apartment was smart with black-and-white prints on the walls, white rugs and black chairs. Julie squatted, cross-legged on a cushion and Diamond took a chair. She wore a wrap tied with a sash at the waist, and he saw hard muscular legs. She didn't seem to have anything on underneath.

'Don't get ideas, brother. I just got out of bed, is all.'

Diamond smiled. 'I'm satisfied with my own woman.'

'Lucky woman . . . say, you scared of snakes?'

'Only the poisonous kind.'

'That's good.' Julie sat motionless as a statue, only her eyes moving towards a corner of the room. 'I shan't have to put Suzie back in her basket. She likes to move around, and that makes some people nervous.'

Diamond glanced over to where she was looking and saw the python slowly slithering across a rug, its head raised. Suzie had a mottled emerald green and brown pattern that glittered in the sunlight coming through the window.

'So what d'you want for your money?'

Diamond reflected that this girl had a unique way of discouraging men who didn't interest her.

'I've a client whose daughter has fallen for Doc Ambrose's line — and he wants her back. Personally, I read Ambrose as no more than a conman and, if you were to tell her, maybe she'll believe you and go back home. I'm offering three-fifty for this service.'

Julie's eyes widened. Her olive skin still held the musky scent of a woman straight from her bed.

'Make it four and I can be very convincing.'

'Done.' Diamond opened his wallet and counted out the bills; he didn't think Leland would baulk at paying if he got Ella back.

Julie rose in one movement, as sinuous as her snake, uncoiling smoothly without using her hands. She counted the money and held on tight to it.

'Tonight at the club,' she said. 'After my act.'

The turf was brown under a hot sun and the ladies sheltered beneath brightly-coloured parasols. In the parade ring, trainers and owners proudly walked their horses to show them to best advantage. The New Orleans racetrack was crowded with holidaymakers and tourists, and noisy with bookies and touts.

Greco, beside Craig Hartmann the bookmaker, leaned on a white-painted rail looking at the horses in the ring with minimum interest. He wasn't concerned with horseflesh, only in fixing races so they made him a profit. He had a share of Hartmann's business.

The bookmaker was broad-shouldered, red-faced, and wore his hair in tight curls; heavy rings sparkled on his fingers as he pointed out a chestnut with a white blaze.

'That's Oriel.'

Greco glanced at the favourite and nodded.

'Unless you can do something, Leon, Oriel is a run-away winner and the betting on him is heavy. Now if he lost, we'd clean up a packet.'

Greco looked around him, at bright silks and grooms and people moving from the grandstand to the bar. He noted Kenny guarding his back, but no one seemed interested in their conversation.

'I can't get at the horse,' Hartmann said. 'Our only chance is the jockey.'

'You've told him I want to speak to him?'

'Yeah. Forry didn't like it much.'

Greco smiled. The jockey would like even less what he had to say.

'Here he comes now . . . '

Forrest was short, thin and bow-legged, his skin lightly tanned. He wore racing colours with a peaked cap and carried a whip, which he tapped against one calf as he walked towards them. He had the rolling gait of a sailor.

'Forry, this is Mr. Greco . . . '

The jockey nodded slightly, his lips taut-pressed into a thin line. Hartmann drifted away, leaving Forrest alone with Greco.

'It's nice to meet a rider who cares about his horse. Mr. Hartmann tells me you always ride Oriel when he's running, that the owner won't put anyone else in the saddle and that you really love that animal.' Greco paused to make a smile. 'So it would be a great pity if anything happened to Oriel.'

Forrest's face turned pale. 'What d'you mean? Nothing's going to happen to him!'

Greco pulled a copy of the Times-Picayune from his pocket, unfolded it and pointed to a short news paragraph. 'I'd like you to read this . . . '

USED CAR DEALER BEATEN UP

Robert Muller was attacked by a man wielding an iron bar and had both legs broken. Recovering in hospital, Muller stated: 'I'd never seen the man before — he didn't want money.' The police have not yet made an arrest.

'So what? I don't see — '

Greco spoke softly. 'It would be a pity if someone used an iron bar on Oriel's legs wouldn't it?'

Forrest gripped his whip till his knuckles blanched. 'Nobody can get near him to do anything like that.'

'Not today, perhaps. Probably not tomorrow either. But can you guard him all the time? Next week? Next month?'

Greco's voice was soft and cajoling. 'You wouldn't really want your horse to suffer because of something you did, would you? Not when you can so easily avoid it. And I promise you it will happen. So Oriel won't win today . . . if you come in a close second, who's to know? Oriel won't be touched and there'll be a bonus for you. Say, five thousand dollars.'

Forrest, almost in tears, turned away.

Greco caught his arm and murmured, 'Don't think Oriel can't be reached. That would be a terrible mistake.'

Forrest said, 'Bastard,' through clenched teeth and stumbled blindly away.

Greco watched him go, smiling, then walked towards the Tote. He queued up at a betting window and put five hundred dollars on the second favourite, Comet, then rejoined Hartmann who looked questioningly at him.

'It'll be all right,' Greco said confidently.

They made their way to the track, near the finishing post as the crowd roared . . . 'They're off!'

Hartmann raised his binoculars and watched the horses race into the curve, jockeying for position. Oriel was among the leaders and going well. Turf flew up from beneath thundering hooves; the sun on the riders' silks dazzled the eyes.

Coming into the finishing straight, Oriel was neck and neck with Comet, both jockeys using their whips. But when it came to the final spurt for victory, Oriel didn't seem quite able to make it and came in second.

Greco smiled at Hartmann and went to collect his winnings. He frowned as a thought crossed his mind: if only it were as easy to fix Diamond. He still hadn't decided exactly how to deal with his ex-enforcer, only that he must. Diamond couldn't be allowed to interfere again.

He strolled to the paddock where Forrest was unsaddling. 'You can have your bonus now if you want,' he said quietly.

The jockey stared wildly at him. 'I don't want your money. Keep it. Just leave my horse alone!'

★ ★ ★

Vallette Street was quiet in the early evening when Diamond parked outside the run-down house where Ella Leland currently resided. Weeds grew around the porch and flakes of paint fell away when he used the doorknocker. He kept on knocking, louder and louder, until someone opened the door.

Then he stepped quickly inside, sniffing the air: grass. He hoped she wasn't high on the stuff.

'I'm calling on Ella,' he announced.

The skinny young man in denim cut-offs and sneakers turned and yelled down the passage: 'Ella . . . company!'

Diamond moved smoothly past him as a door opened and Ella Leland's head poked out. Her expression changed to disgust. 'You again. Don't you ever give up?'

Diamond gave her his best smile. He was wearing a casual suit in light tan with a silk tie. 'I'm offering dinner and a show.'

'Yeah?' She was immediately suspicious. 'Why?'

'Because I want you to meet someone. No harm in that, is there?'

'Depends who it is.'

'Her name's Julie. She's the dancer you saw at Doc Ambrose's the other night.'

'Why?' Ella seemed genuinely puzzled,

'I'd like you to see her in her natural habitat. You might learn something. After all, you've never had to work, and Julie's strictly a working girl. Or don't you think your new belief can take it?'

Ella smiled grimly at the challenge. 'Okay, big boy, you can buy me dinner.'

'It would be nice if you wore a dress.'

'Maybe I should get a perm too? And take a bath?'

Diamond grinned. 'Why not?'

'If you want to wait, wait.'

The door closed in his face and Diamond located a chair in the unlit hallway and sat down. He thought Ella might tell him to go to hell but he didn't think she was the sort to sneak out the back way.

The skinny young man who'd let him in drifted by. 'You want a smoke, man?'

'Thanks, but no. I don't use the stuff.'

The hall was a drab brown that obviously hadn't been decorated for years. Someone had made a half-hearted attempt to wash the grime off one side, and given up. It was a depressing place.

A couple of girls in skin-tight jeans, bra-less under skimpy T-shirts wiggled past him on their way out. Nice enough kids, Diamond thought; they'd straighten out — unless some pusher got them on a downward spiral to oblivion.

He didn't grieve over Earl Vogel's death — though his pride was hurt — but he was puzzled by it. Cave had set him up — and then got him off the hook in the lieutenant's office. None of it made sense.

When Ella Leland appeared, she wore a neat blue gown with her hair brushed and carried a handbag. Diamond got to his feet.

'Reckon I'll pass inspection?'

'Reckon you look pretty when you take

the trouble,' Diamond said gallantly. 'That's a nice perfume too. It's a real pleasure to be your escort.'

They went out to his Mustang and he drove across the bridge from Algiers and turned right to head towards the French Quarter.

'Where are we going?'

'The *Folies Club*.'

'I've never been there.'

He parked on Bourbon and they walked the rest of the way. The *Folies* glittered like tinsel as they went through the doorway; lights sparkled and a jazz band was playing around with *Limehouse Blues*. The atmosphere was totally different from daytime.

'I booked by phone,' Diamond said. 'A table for two.'

'Yes sir. This way, please.'

They were seated and studied the menu; Ella ordered a seafood platter, and Diamond steak with salad. He asked for a bottle of wine, but only sipped from his glass.

The lighting was discreet, the tables grouped about a small square of floor where couples danced. Ella ate as though she hadn't tasted decent food in a long time. She emptied her glass and Diamond refilled it, humming along with the band.

She was studying him closely. 'Are you married, Mr. Diamond?'

'My friends call me Wash and, no, I'm not exactly married. My girl friend's a professional singer and very independently minded.'

'For a cop, you're not all bad,' Ella admitted grudgingly.

'What I really wanted to be is a jazz trumpeter. I'm just not good enough.'

'Modest, too.'

Diamond thought she was a pleasant enough girl but, because her family had money, she'd never had to tough it out. With her fair hair, freckles and boyish figure, she was an innocent compared to Chelsea or Julie.

The band finished its number and cleared the stage. The lights dimmed and a spotlight shone on the empty dance floor. A sleek man in a tuxedo appeared from the side to announce:

'Ladies and gentlemen. Our cabaret

star this evening is Julie, direct from the voodoo cults of the Congo. Give her a great welcome, please.'

When the clapping died away, hidden drums beat slowly, softly as Julie glided onstage, the python already wound about her shoulders. The rhythm remained languorous as the drums beat louder. Julie's dance was different from the one she'd performed at Doc Ambrose's temple; only her hips seemed to move as the snake slithered lower about her body. And she wore a figure-fitting sheath.

She swayed to the drumbeat, juggling Suzie as she reached behind for the zipper of her dress. Gradually the sheath slipped away from her shoulders. She paused, eyes downcast, peeking sideways over her shoulder at the men ogling her. Then the sheath fell away and she stepped out of it.

The drumbeat softened, quickened a little. Suzie coiled about her waist, head lifting as she reached up to unclip and release her bra.

The lighting changed kaleidoscopically. Julie's hips, clad in lace panties, gyrated as she eased the python up around her shoulders. The audience held its breath as her fingers slid beneath the elastic at her waist.

Where her performance for Doc Ambrose had climaxed in a religious ecstasy, her strip routine was sexually arousing.

The music pulsed faster. Suzie slithered across her breasts.

Julie dropped her last garment as the drums crashed. For a brief instant the spot centred on her, then went out, plunging the stage into darkness.

When the house lights came the stage was deserted.

'Not bad,' Diamond said, admiringly.

'Cheap,' Ella snorted, 'after her real performance.' She sounded bitter, as if a dent had been made in her newfound belief.

Diamond rose from his chair. 'Come on, I'll take you backstage to meet her.'

'Suppose I don't want to?'

'What are you scared of? She's a cabaret artiste, that's all. It might even be interesting for you — I guess you never had to earn your keep, like most girls.'

Ella couldn't resist the challenge; she followed him through a curtained doorway and along a passage. The manager interposed himself smoothly. 'Can I help you?'

'Julie's expecting us.'

The manager tapped lightly on a dressing room door. 'You expecting anyone?'

'Yeah. Show 'em in.'

Diamond entered, followed — a trifle reluctantly — by Ella. The manager closed the door.

'Hi,' Julie said, flashing a smile. She had put on a wrap that gaped revealingly as she bent over to coil her python into a wicker basket. 'I have to keep Suzie shut up or we'll have a panic on our hands. She has a habit of disappearing to explore.'

'Miss Leland is particularly interested in your voodoo dance,' Diamond said. 'She caught your act the other night at Doc Ambrose's temple.'

Julie made a face as she sat down before the dressing table mirror. 'That phony! I don't mind doing an act for him, but when I think of all the money he's taking off the suckers, I want to spit.'

Ella said, coldly, 'Just what do you mean by that?'

Julie glanced at her, and laughed. 'What do I mean? I mean he asked me to help out with his voodoo racket — and I assure you he knows even less about the religious aspect than I do — and like one of the mugs he's busy fleecing, I agreed. D'you know what he pays me? Less than half I get for doing a strip here, where I don't have to pretend it's anything more than an act.'

Ella's lips firmed and her face turned a pale shade of grey.

'And his life style! He's got a real elegant house in the Garden District, complete with servants. He does right for himself, does Doc. But voodoo? He'd run a mile if the real thing caught up with him. He's coining money as fast as the staff can take it out of the suckers' pockets. Some religion, huh? Is that the sort of thing you want to hear? I can sure tell you a lot more.'

Ella made her way blindly to the door, fighting back tears.

Julie winked at Diamond as he went after her.

Outside on the sidewalk, Ella burst out: 'Well, say it. Say you told me so. You can laugh if you want — I don't have anything left. Ambrose really had me believing those things he preached were true.'

Diamond caught her in his arms and held her close.

'I'll tell you what's true, Ella. Your father cares about you, and some girls aren't so lucky.'

12

Southern Comfort

On the stage Chelsea Hull, wearing a flame-red gown and cradling the micro-phone to her lips, tapped out the rhythm as she sang:

'Just as blue as blue can be
'Cause my man's gone 'way from me
Gone 'way, long way 'way
Got dem blues by night and day.'

It was early in the evening and the tables were half-empty so she easily spotted Cave when he came into the *Black Cat*. She recognized him from Wash's description and was surprised and apprehensive and wondered what he wanted.

The detective bought himself a beer at the bar, tossed his Panama onto an empty table and sat down. He took a mouthful of beer, looked around him with a pained expression and lit a cigarette.

When her number ended, he waved her across. Chelsea, reluctant but curious, joined him at his table. His corrugated face grimaced as Joe and his band swung into *Chinatown*.

'What's the matter? Don't you like what I sing?'

'You don't have a bad voice,' Cave admitted sourly. 'It's just that jazz isn't my kind of music.'

'Oh, and what is your kind of music?'

'Chopin, Bach, Vivaldi . . . that sort of thing, you know.' Abruptly he changed the subject. 'Where's the big fellar tonight?'

'Trying to persuade an erring daughter to return home.' Chelsea kept her tone light; she didn't want her hostility showing. This honky was a cop and she was scared he was setting Wash up for something bad; already he'd nearly got her man killed. She didn't trust him. 'Why?'

'Just checking.'

Chelsea pressed, 'Is Wash going to stay with this P.I. job?'

Cave swallowed beer and burped. 'Who

knows? He's shaping up, but it's early days yet. 'It's better than enforcing for Greco. We'll have to wait and see how he handles himself when the chips are down.'

★　★　★

Greco stepped from the shower cubicle, towelled himself dry and leisurely dressed in fresh underwear. His pale flesh was flushed and his brain active.

He felt hamstrung with Turk in hiding; without an enforcer, he knew damn well people were ripping him off. But he didn't want to set Kenny on them. That meant killing, and he couldn't afford a lot of heat from the cops at the present time.

He slipped into a pale grey shirt, looked at his face in the mirror and saw the start of bags forming under his eyes. And getting a paunch too. It worried him that he was beginning to feel his years. Earlier, he'd have toughed it out himself; now he had to rely on others. If that fool Diamond hadn't quit on him, there wouldn't be this trouble . . .

He adjusted his pants and knotted a tie. Who the hell did Wash think he was anyway? A muscleman, too smart for his own good.

Greco put on his jacket and checked his pockets. There was nothing to worry about with Vogel; his lawyer had managed to stop any questioning of Kenny. That was okay, but it bothered him the cops had even tried it on.

And all because of Diamond. Well, he had to be wiped out and that was definite.

Maybe his other managers would take the hint and cool it when word got around that Wash had been taken out.

Who to give the job to? Not Kenny — too obvious. And certainly not anyone on his new agency list. It had to be an outsider . . .

'Are you going to be all day, Leon?'

Barbara sounded impatient.

'Just finished.'

He selected a clean handkerchief and strolled into the bedroom.

Barbara, at twenty-eight, had a statuesque figure and rarely wore clothes in her apartment. Cigarette stuck in one corner of her mouth, she swept past him and into the shower stall. She worked in TV advertising, collected good money and was something of a sexual athlete.

Her apartment was both luxurious and sensual, personally designed for her by a top interior decorator. Greco felt good. Barbara usually had that effect on him, though he wasn't all that interested these days. He could go a long time between women. He supposed he continued only to protect his macho image; it wouldn't do for word to get around that Leon Greco was reluctant to service a woman.

Diamond now . . . there was a name nagging at the back of his mind. He lit a cigar and stood by the window, looking out across Lake Pontchartrain on the northern edge of New Orleans. Beyond the trees and benches, people sunbathed on the beach. He saw the causeway crossing the lake and the boats; he liked watching the boats. Maybe he'd buy one when he got settled; his mind worked subconsciously . . . boats . . . water . . . swamp . . . Cajun country. And the name came to him. Haggar.

His memory flashed back to a time soon after he'd moved south, before he hired Kenny, when he was looking for a bodyguard. 'Beau' Haggar had been mentioned. He'd met the man, a hard-line Southerner and member of the KKK, a genuine fire-breathing black-hater. He'd sooner kill a black man than spit on him.

At that time, Greco had ducked out; he didn't want a crazy man, a hater. A man like that wasn't safe, couldn't be trusted to stay cool.

But Diamond was a negro; for a one-off, it was the perfect set-up. Greco smiled as he phoned Kenny to bring the car round. He didn't wait for Barbara to finish her shower, just called a goodbye and took the elevator down.

He got in the back of the Ford and gave Kenny directions. Away from the city, on Route 90, Kenny moved into top gear, muttering away as he lived his latest sex fantasy.

Beyond the suburbs, it didn't take long to reach Cajun country; the low flat delta was a land of cypress swamp and marsh, evergreen and magnolia, a tangle of vegetation that harboured alligators.

Haggar had a place off the highway and when Kenny turned off, the Ford bumped slowly along a dirt track. There was no sign of habitation and nobody about. It was like driving through a jungle.

After half-an-hour, Greco said, 'Here,' and Kenny stopped outside a pine cabin; most of the paint had long since peeled away till the place looked derelict. Haggar made his money as a hunter and lived alone; he didn't mind roughing it.

Greco got out of the car into a sticky heat, the air smelling vile from the muddy delta water alongside the cabin, and walked towards the sagging porch.

Beauregard Haggar sat in an old cane chair, taking his ease on the veranda and sipping from a dirty glass. A .22 rifle, oiled and spotless, leaned against the wooden wall beside him. The weapon was cleaner than Haggar or his cabin; it was the only possession he took any trouble over. He was unshaven, his whiskers sprouting in uneven bristles, and he smelt almost as bad as the marsh.

His voice was a nasal Southern whine. 'I ain't taking no one a-hunting today, so you can just turn around and go home, Mister City Slicker.'

Greco moved up onto the veranda out of the sun, taking care where he placed his expensive highly polished shoes; there was dogshit everywhere and the boards didn't seem any too safe. An evil-looking hound padded up, baring yellow teeth.

'If'n I tell Pooch to take a bite of yuh, you-all'll run fast enough,' Beau Haggar drawled and took another sip from his glass.

'I want you to hunt down a black for me,' Greco said quietly. 'I want you to kill him. I'll pay you five thousand dollars when he's dead.'

Haggar's eyes gleamed and he sat up straight in his chair and reached for his rifle. 'Ain't no black worth that much, but you've surely got me interested.'

'Take care,' Greco warned. 'I've a man in the car.'

Haggar spat and set down his empty

glass. 'Show you what Ah'll do to that black of your'n,' he grunted and raised the rifle butt to his shoulder. 'You hear that bird? Mockingbird.'

Greco turned to where the rifle pointed and saw, about two hundred yards away, a bird perched on the branch of a tree, half-screened by leaves.

Haggar took aim, almost caressing his rifle as he took first pressure.

'Never give a black an even break,' he cackled as he squeezed off a shot.

The mockingbird fell out of the tree into the undergrowth.

'His name's Diamond,' Greco said, impressed. 'And I can tell you where to find him.'

Haggar smiled and lowered the rifle. 'Won't take but a moment to turn him into a good black — a dead one.'

Greco extracted ten twenties from his wallet. 'For expenses.'

A hand like a claw reached for the money and tucked it into the pocket of a faded shirt. Beau Haggar poured himself another drink.

'Reckon you got yourself a deal, Mister.

My pleasure — that black of your'n's good as spitted.'

★   ★   ★

Diamond walked back to the office from his bank with a feeling of satisfaction. He'd just paid in the cheque Leland had sent him. If business held up, he might make a go of the investigation business.

The latest issue of Yellow Pages had arrived and he turned immediately to the entry for Detective Agencies:

WASHINGTON T. DIAMOND
All investigations including:
Tracing Missing Persons
Bodyguarding
Confidential Investigations
Security

He put his feet on the desk, grinning broadly, and watched the tourists pass by on the other side of the street. He thought of the coming Sunday morning when he had a date with Chelsea at a black church. It was not often they could arrange to attend together and join in the gospel singing; that was something they both enjoyed.

He ought to make time to get to a gym for a workout; he couldn't afford to let himself get out of condition . . .

The telephone rang. 'Diamond.'

'Ah need help.' The voice at the other end of the line held a Southern whine.

'What kind of help?'

'I ain't saying nothing on an open line. You-all ready to meet me?'

'Just say when and where.'

'I'll be waiting on Front Street. There's this parking lot with a pay booth opposite a barber's shop. Nine o'clock tonight.'

'How will I know you?'

'Don't worry yourself — sure reckon Ah'll know you.'

'Okay, I'll be there,' Diamond said, and the line went dead.

He looked at his watch. He had time to jog around the three-mile circuit at Audubon Park.

★   ★   ★

Beauregard Haggar smiled unpleasantly in the shadow of an upstairs room on Front Street. He cradled his .22 in his arms as he waited, with the loving care a mother gives her first-born. Lights from a distant warehouse cast a yellow glow over the riverfront and he had an unobstructed view of the car park and the telephone booth. There were few people about.

He took a quick swallow from the bottle of whisky standing on the bare boards beside him. The room was empty and dusty and hadn't been in use for a long time.

Diamond was a big man, a target he couldn't miss. He'd stationed himself opposite the Coin-Op place on Orleans when Diamond went in by the side door, so he'd have no difficulty recognizing him.

Haggar wondered idly why Greco wanted him dead, but wasn't really interested. A black was a black and one less made the world a better place in his opinion; it was just unfortunate that the law wasn't as easy-going as it once had been. He could remember when the Klan would stage a lynching and the law looked the other way . . .

Like the time they dressed up in white sheets and hoods, all armed with shotguns and carrying a fiery cross. They'd surrounded this shack out in the boondocks, drunk as lords and passing the bottle from hand to hand. Buckshot kept the blacks inside and the cross set the place alight. He remembered the stink of burning bodies as the shack blazed like a tarpaper torch, the screams . . .

But times were changing. He recalled Greco now and was vaguely aware he'd made his way to the top of the heap; likely he'd have a high-priced lawyer in tow in case anything went wrong.

Haggar lifted his rifle and sighted on the target area. No problem, one clean shot — he couldn't miss at this range — and out the back way. This was going to be the easiest money he'd ever made.

Diamond must really be getting under Greco's skin for him to pay two thousand bucks to get rid of him. Haggar hadn't said so, but he'd have made the kill for free. God, how he hated those uppity black slaves swaggering about as if they owned the country, raping white women; it was enough to give a man blood pressure.

He waited, watching the evening shadows grow. The time was close on nine.

He took another swig from the bottle — good stuff, paid for with Greco's expense money. Not the cheap booze he often had to put up with. Swamp hunting wasn't all that great these days.

The minutes dragged by and he became impatient as he looked from the open window.

'Come on, you black bastard, come and get it.'

★   ★   ★

Daylight was fading from the sky as Diamond drove down Poydras Street and turned right onto Front. The lights of the revolving bar on top of the Trade Mart were behind him and across the river, black and mysterious, Algiers showed as a regular grid of yellow oblongs. He glimpsed the shadowy outlines of grain barges.

He glanced at his watch; he was early and slowed, wondering what sort of job it was this time. It had been a local voice, not a tourist. Did the man realize he was black and would that make any difference? Some of the old-time Southerners still lived in the past.

He didn't have far to go. He saw the parking lot ahead and turned in. The phone booth was empty. There was a vacant row of shops opposite, looking as if they were waiting to be torn down for rebuilding. The whole area seemed not only deserted, but derelict.

A faint light shone from a warehouse further along the waterfront. The evening was still and quiet with only distant traffic sounds as he got out of the Mustang and closed the door.

He stood looking about him. There was no sign of his client and he walked towards the telephone booth; perhaps the client was going to ring to make another rendezvous.

Diamond felt alone in the world, and

scarily conspicuous. For no obvious reason the hairs on the back of his neck bristled. An old instinct was warning him, as it had more than once in his army days, and he quickened his pace across the deserted lot. He remembered Earl Vogel being gunned down and headed for the nearest patch of shadow.

He almost made it.

He heard the crack of a rifle and staggered as something hit and spun him around. He fell, feeling a trickle of blood under his shirt, rolled into deep shadow and lay still.

13

Quick Burner

The Kingfisher Conference Centre lay between Highway Ten and the Mississippi, midway between New Orleans and Baton Rouge, capital of Louisiana. When Madden discovered it, the place had obviously seen better times. He assumed it had paid its way before the Hilton and other big hotels took the convention business to New Orleans.

Madden liked it as soon as he set eyes on the low rambling buildings set in their own grounds. There was a small conference room set apart from the main centre, with residential apartments close by. All nicely tucked away from curious eyes.

When he'd enquired the hiring fee, the manager had shown a moment's embarrassment despite his obvious eagerness.

'Business has been slow, sir, which

172

means we've had to let some of our staff go. Of course, I can get new people — '

Smiling, Madden shook his head. 'That's not necessary. Ours will be a small business meeting, a handful of executives only. I represent Apex Industrials — from the west coast — and we're about to market a new product. This is one of a few areas designated to test the product. So, we don't need a lot of extra people running around. Confidential is the word.'

The manager looked shocked. 'I assure you, sir — all our conferences are strictly private.'

'And that's the way we want it. Mustn't let our competitors get a smell of this before it's too late for them to catch up.' Madden winked. 'My sales force can rough it for a week or so, long enough to get our marketing organised . . . '

Now Madden smiled at the recollection as he stood at one side of a flat table covered by a large scale map. It showed the objective, a grid of roads, the main highway and University building, the river and steamboat jetty.

'Everything clear? Any questions?'

Across the table, five men sat on folding chairs studying the layout. They were completely absorbed, their faces serious.

'Nobody carries a gun on this job,' Madden repeated. 'The operation will go smoothly providing no one loses his cool.'

Blackie Hendriks, uncomfortable in a business suit, screwed up his face in thought. 'Only the one guard?'

'Only one. And he's middle-aged, sensible — not the sort to play at being a hero. We'll have complete surprise. All attention will be on Fisher when he makes his announcement — you just take his gun away from him.'

'How much?' Woody asked. He was tall and thick as a tree with rust-coloured hair now tinged with grey.

'The last weekend of the month they have to carry a lot of cash to cover salaries. My best estimate is between four hundred thousand and a half a million.'

'Cars?'

Madden looked at Skip, the number

two driver. 'You and Ted find your own. Nothing hot.'

'Violets', squat and powerful, brooded and said nothing.

Madden's cool grey eyes surveyed his team with satisfaction. Greco had done a good job of recruitment. These calm men were all professionals, calm and watchful.

Casually, he asked: 'Is that it?'

There was silence in the conference room except for some heavy breathing.

'Right then,' Madden said, rolling up the map. 'It's on.'

★ ★ ★

Diamond lay motionless, letting his breath out in one long easy sigh and listening intently. He had a moment of déja vu when he could smell dank undergrowth, almost see the Viet Cong sniper high among vivid green foliage. He desperately wanted a Browning Automatic Rifle and a couple of grenades. He listened for a tell-tale rustle of leaves.

Then the jungle vision faded and he was lying on tarmac, in shadow, on a parking lot on Front Street in New Orleans. He saw a crumpled plastic bag, smelt stale beer from an empty can and tobacco from a discarded cigarette pack.

Hell, he'd gone through a war without getting shot . . .

The shock and numbness faded and the pain started, high up in his left side; his arm felt useless and blood glued the shirt to his skin. Only a flesh wound, he told himself; he'd been lucky.

He waited. The tarmac felt gritty under his hands. No further shot came and there was no movement across the empty lot. He had the sniper's position pin-pointed now; an open window on the second floor of an empty barber's shop. A faded sign read:

ERNIE'S
Shave and Trim

Someone had set him up and it wasn't Ernie. He was safe in dark shadow as long as he didn't move; any movement might attract another bullet.

He began to shiver and knew he was

losing blood; he had to get his wound attended to as soon as possible. And that meant he had to move, knowing that a revolver was no match against a rifle.

Fear made his flesh crawl. Had the would-be killer gone? Or was he still up there, waiting for his target to move into the light?

He looked towards his Mustang; there was only one other car in the lot, a wreck that had been dumped. Diamond eased himself off the ground, crouching and drawing his revolver with his right hand. He watched the window opposite; it remained dark and blank as if it were laughing at him. Must be getting light-headed, he thought — windows don't laugh.

Move it, soldier!

He ran a fast zigzagging course across the tarmac, ending up close to the door of the barber's shop, breathing hard. He waited, listening, getting his breath back. There was no sound from inside and he tried the door; it opened with a squeal of hinges.

He kicked it wide, went inside fast and

slammed his back against a wall, revolver held at chest level.

Nobody took a shot at him. He listened again; still there was no sound. Then his eyes adjusted to the gloom, he saw bare boards and dust, a grimy plate window and a pile of rubbish in the far corner.

Faint scuffmarks indicated where someone had gone upstairs. He crossed to the bottom of the staircase and peered out into darkness. Silence lingered. He took the stairs at a rush and arrived at a landing with a short passage. One room at the front and one at the back. At the end of the passage, a fire door was swinging half-open.

Diamond was almost sure the rifleman had gone, but he stayed wary. He kicked open the front room door and smelt cordite. There was a brass shell on the floorboards, otherwise the room was empty.

He pocketed the shell and checked the back room. No one.

He walked along the passage to the fire door and looked down a flight of rusting iron steps. There was no sign of the would-be assassin; he had got clean away.

Diamond returned to his car and drove slowly, one-handed, to the nearest hospital and walked into Emergency. The duty intern removed his coat, cut away his shirt and washed off the blood. He took a careful look.

'You realize we have to notify the police in the event of a gunshot wound?'

Diamond felt drained of energy. 'I imagine so,' he said wearily. 'See if you can get hold of Detective Cave — he knows me.'

'Will do. You're a lucky man. The bullet went straight through, missing the bone, so you're just missing a chunk of flesh. It'll be sore as hell for a few days, but you'll live.'

The intern swabbed the wound with antiseptic and bandaged his arm.

'Now I want you to take it easy, just stay sitting a while. Shock can do funny things to the nervous system.'

As he walked off to deal with the next patient, a nurse brought Diamond a mug of hot sweet tea.

'Drink this, and we'll see how you feel later on.'

Diamond sipped the tea uneasily, acutely aware of the blanketing smell of antiseptic and the way it made his stomach heave. He put his feet up and his head back, trying to ignore the pain in his arm as he drowsily wondered who the rifleman had been.

He was dropping off to sleep when Cave arrived. The Detective's wrinkled face was beaming and he lit a Marlboro with a flourish.

'So we spooked the Fox into action! The lieutenant got nowhere on the Vogel killing — Greco had his lawyer primed and ready. And Turk's gone undercover. It looks like he's reacting to pressure. So what have you got for me?'

Diamond handed him the shell he'd picked up. 'He used a rifle.'

'Where was this?'

Cave listened to his story without interruption.

'Yeah, well, next time you'll know better than to agree to a blind date. What was his voice like?'

'White, southern. One of the good old boys.'

'They're still with us. I'll phone for a car to take a look at that barber's — you never know, we might get lucky.'

When he returned, Cave asked: 'D'you want to stay here tonight? I can fix it for you — and it might be safer.'

'No way.' Diamond climbed unsteadily to his feet. 'It's only a flesh wound and I'm going home.'

Cave shrugged. 'Okay, it's your life. I'll drive you back.'

They went outside to his car. The detective took it slowly even though traffic was light. He crossed Canal and headed east along Royal, past darkened shops. Sirens wailed and cars piled up. Traffic got so bad, Cave had to pull over.

He frowned. 'Looks as though this is as far as we go. You fit enough to walk the rest? Figure I ought to investigate this jam.'

Diamond nodded and got out of the Plymouth and, together, they followed the crowd.

'Jackals,' Cave muttered, and asked one

of the crowd: 'What's going on?'

'A fire, man!'

Turning into Orleans Avenue, they saw red fire engines, pumps and ladders, trailing hoses like spaghetti. The gutters were awash with water as firemen played their jets on the buildings. Police held back the crowd. Diamond and Cave edged forward. Smoke hung like fog in the air and there was a smell of burning.

They paused as they caught a glimpse of the Coin-Op Laundromat; the building was a shell, gutted by fire and the firemen were concentrating on saving the adjacent buildings. It was immediately obvious that Diamond no longer had an office or a room to sleep in.

'Wait here,' Cave said, and bulled his way through to the fire chief, flashing his I.D.

He spoke briefly and his face was set when he returned. 'Someone sure don't like you, Wash. Arson is suspected. The chief says it looks like a petrol bomb was used.'

14

'Queen of the South'

Haggar tipped up the whisky bottle and swallowed as he listened to the telephone ringing at the far end of the line. He peered out through the dirty glass of the call booth at the motel reception hall. It was empty apart from the night clerk at his desk; even the lighting was subdued. Beyond the glass front he glimpsed the dark silhouettes of look-alike cabins.

This was the third number he had tried to get hold of Leon Greco; that man surely moved around some, but Haggar was in no hurry. He'd booked in at a cheap motel on the outskirts of the city, a temporary base, and his old station wagon was parked out of sight at the rear.

A neutral voice said, 'Greco.'

'Beau here. I only winged your black bird. He moved just as — '

'Christ!' Greco exploded. 'Am I sur-rounded by total incompetents?'

'No sir, you are not.' Haggar spoke with convincing earnestness. 'That man has the luck of the devil himself — but Ah never gives up on a black, that's something you can rely on. For certain sure I'll keep after him.

'It's this way now — he no longer has an office. Just a little trick I learnt to keep the quarry from cover. You-all know any place he might hole up?'

Haggar listened to quiet breathing, then —

'He has a girlfriend, Chelsea something or other, a singer at the *Black Swan* club, off Bourbon. He plays trumpet some-times. He'll show up there.'

'That's Jim and Dandy, Mr. Greco. I'll check on the bitch. You relax now, and start counting all that lovely money you're going to pay me.'

* * *

Diamond stood looking at the burnt-out frame of his temporary home, anger building in him, his one good hand tightly clenched. He wanted to hit out at someone, preferably Greco.

'Sure looks like you've needled the Fox,' Cave said. 'I reckon we might just catch him off-balance now.'

Diamond said suddenly: 'Chelsea! I've got to make sure she's all right.'

They forced a way through the crowd, back to Cave's Plymouth. A traffic jam had built up, horns blaring, but the detective flashed his badge and a patrolman eased him out into the flow.

'Have to go the long way round,' he grunted, picking up speed. He detoured by way of St. Peter Street and Chartres to the apartment house on Esplanade.

'Seems quiet enough,' Cave said as they pounded up the stairs and Diamond leaned on the bell push.

When the door opened on a chain, Diamond asked quickly: 'You okay? No trouble?'

'I'm fine,' Chelsea said, unhooking the chain. Her eyes widened. 'What happened to you?'

'It's nothing, baby. A scratch.'

Chelsea was in a wrap, getting ready for bed when Diamond and Cave walked in. She made more tea for Wash and got a beer from the fridge for Cave, and listened to what they had to say.

Her lips tightened. 'This is your fault,' she accused the detective.

Cave pulled the tab on his can and swallowed, wiped his mouth with the back of his hand. 'Blame Greco, if you want to blame anybody.'

Chelsea made a wry face. 'So much for fame,' she said. 'I guess my portrait burnt up with the building. So it's lucky you left your trumpet with me — and the rest of your clothes.'

Cave lit a cigarette. 'My advice is to get out of town and take your girlfriend with you. Greco must know you shack up here.'

'I'm not running,' Diamond said stubbornly. 'I'm going after him.'

Cave's laugh turned into a fit of coughing. When he recovered, he jeered: 'Don't make me laugh. A black kills a white man — what chance d'you think you'd have? I know times have changed, but not that much. So cool it and wait till I set something up.'

'The way you set Wash up?' Chelsea said tartly.

'Yeah, just like that. And don't think I can't do it, lady. I set one up, I can set up two.'

He swallowed more beer.

'I don't go for this crap about criminals being the fault of society, or any of the other psychiatric-liberal bullshit. I believe criminals are scum, that they hurt people because they enjoy it, that they rob the weak and the old because it's easier than work. I hate them. I believe they should be shot down like mad dogs.'

He took a last drag on his Marlboro and ground out the butt with a savage twist of his wrist, as if demonstrating, and rose to his feet.

'Now get the hell out of this town, will ya? Keep in touch by phone — ' He scribbled a number on a notepad, tore off the page and thrust it at Diamond. 'Ill let you know when and where to find Greco. And I'll put a couple of cops outside, one back and front, though I don't reckon we'll see any more action tonight.'

After he had left, Chelsea said, 'He's right, Wash. Greco's got an organisation and you're only one man. And look what he's done already — you got shot and burnt out. I'm scared.'

'You don't have to be scared while I'm here.'

Diamond checked the doors and windows, dragged a couch across the doorway and stretched out, revolver in one big black hand.

'You can sleep sound, baby.'

'Tomorrow,' Chelsea said firmly, 'We're getting out, like that detective told us.' She switched off the light and went into the bedroom.

Diamond lay listening to apartment house sounds. Eventually it grew quiet but he couldn't drop off to sleep. He felt restless, his injured arm was uncomfortable and his brain went round and round as he thought up unpleasant things to do to Leon Greco when he got his hands on him. The moon shone through the window. He heard a car speed by, a distant clock strike twice, then he must have dozed off because he smelt coffee and when he raised his head, sunlight blinded him.

He heard Chelsea talking on the telephone, a note of urgency in her voice. 'Okay, okay I'll take it. Two o'clock. I'll be there.'

She replaced the receiver, turned and saw he was awake. 'Move, Wash. Shower, and I'll change that dressing, then breakfast. We're getting out of here.'

'Where you planning on going?'

'I've got a job on a riverboat. And there's a chance for you to sit in with Vince's band. The main thing is we'll be out of town for a few days — and no one will find it easy to reach you in the middle of the river.'

'That's smart thinking, baby.'

He found himself a new shirt and put his bloodstained jacket on one side to go to the cleaners.

After a breakfast of ham and hot sausage, he said: 'I'll meet you at the quayside. I want to collect my car.'

He took a Yellow cab to the hospital, drove his car to the nearest garage and left it for servicing. The sidewalks were filling with people and he felt less conspicuous now. As he walked down Common Street towards the waterfront he was conscious that somewhere, a man with a rifle might be stalking him; he was glad that he'd put on a tan suit and grey shirt rather than his usual bright colours.

When he reached the quay at the foot of Canal, tourists were going up the gangway onto the sternwheeler, looking happy and relaxed and in vacation mood.

Chelsea was waiting on the top deck with his trumpet, and introduced him to Vince Norman. The bandleader wore a baggy linen suit that resembled a collapsed parachute, and his face beamed.

'Glad to have you sit in, man. An extra trumpet's always welcome on these outdoor gigs. The sound kinda gets lost, ya know.'

At two o'clock, engines throbbing, gangway aboard and ropes cast off, the *Queen of the South* sounded her siren, sending gulls aloft in a noisy cloud. Paddles churning, the riverboat eased out from the bank and began fighting the current as she headed upstream.

'Right,' Norman said, and tapped his foot, 'One, two, three . . . ' and Diamond raised his trumpet and blew his heart out with the *St. Louis Blues*.

The city skyline passed, a panorama of docks and barges and skyscrapers, and then they were gliding through the suburbs, moving towards open countryside, the deck throbbing and hot music belting out.

Diamond lowered his trumpet after one chorus; he had problems playing with one good hand. But he was grinning in the hot sunshine; he'd never played on a riverboat before and already he was liking it. As good as a holiday while his arm mended. He'd miss the Gospel singing with Chelsea, but there'd be other Sundays.

And he'd be back. He had a score to settle with Leon Greco.

★   ★   ★

Beau Haggar walked the streets of New Orleans and didn't like what he saw; it was quite a while since he'd visited the city and things had obviously got worse. Blacks didn't get off the sidewalk when he approached. And when he saw one arm-in-arm with a white woman, his vision blurred as if he was seeing through a blood-red veil. He kept his temper only because he knew he had to. With two thousand dollars involved, he couldn't afford trouble. He had to pick up Diamond's trail again.

Greco had said his girlfriend was a singer at a jazz club and he was on his way there now. He ground his teeth; he'd have to talk politely to the brothers to get information when he'd sooner stamp them into the ground. Then he laughed aloud as the thought struck him — he was going to get one black to betray another. And that was fine and dandy.

He found the *Black Swan* open even though it was midday, and heard the sound of a band practising. He strode in as if he owned the building, and stopped dead. The band was white.

Haggar softened his approach. He could lie when it suited him. He addressed a musician who was sitting out, fitting a new reed to his instrument.

'Ah'm looking for a singer name o' Chelsea. Maybe you-all can toll me where she might be?'

The musician's gaze flicked over him; he wasn't upset by the questioner's looks — jazz fans came in all shapes and sizes.

'Well now, she's a regular here with Joe Baker's outfit, but I just heard she's away on a river gig.'

'Sure would like to catch her,' Haggar drawled, happy to have the man betray her.

'The boat's the *Queen of the South* and she's with Vince's band. She sails at two, so you'd best hurry, man.'

'I'll do that,' Haggar said, and left.

He hurried through the narrow streets of the French Quarter, down to the quayside; when he arrived, the steamboat had already sailed. He obtained her route and timetable from a small office on the quay, collected his station wagon and set off along the river bank.

He had his rifle with him, cleaned and loaded and he smiled as he drove along.

There was nothing better than black-hunting and he'd flushed his quarry into the open. It was a sure bet that Diamond was with her; why else would she change her job? He'd winged Diamond he knew; it was just bad luck he had moved at the moment he squeezed his trigger — or he'd be a goner right now. Well, this time he'd make sure of him.

Haggar's wagon moved along smoothly. It was old and dirty, but he looked after the engine. He was in no great hurry as he out the city behind him. The paddle steamer couldn't disappear; all he had to do was follow the river till he sighted her, then tag along until he got his chance at Diamond. And all the time they were moving towards the type of country he knew best.

Two thousand bucks to enjoy himself. Could be he'd knock off the brownskin gal too; two for the price of one. And just maybe he'd get a bit of fun with her first.

An hour later, he sighted the riverboat, paddles churning up white water as she fought the swift-flowing current, and laughed.

The *Queen of the South* moved steadily up the Mississippi, engines pulsing, paddles scooping up water. The top deck was thronged with couples dancing to the hot jazz of Vince Norman's band; coloured lights hung in festoons and laughter carried far across the water.

Sunset made a dull red glow over the bayous as Diamond caught the signal to sit in. He brought up the horn to his lips; his left arm was still stiff and awkward but there was nothing wrong with the fingers of his right hand on the valves. It was great to be playing outdoors, cruising up the river; and he was hitting the notes with vitality and drive, following Chelsea's melodic line:

'Feeling blue, ma man ain't true,
Same old blues, sure get to me
Like a-drowning in the sea.'

It was a happy, relaxed time and, after their number ended, Diamond and Chelsea leaned on the deck rail and watched the dark land glide past. In the twilight Diamond sighted what appeared to be grey logs floating on the surface of the bayou, and suddenly realized they were alligators and shivered. At that moment he was reminded of the jungle.

A smell of brackish water drifted on the evening air and silver-grey tufts of Spanish moss swayed from the oaks. A string of barges came downstream, pushed by a tugboat. Behind them, Vince led the band into *Bugle Call Rag*, his horn swinging hard.

The river was wide and deep and the current flowed strongly, and the *Queen of the South* made slow headway against it. On the bank, cars sped along the highway, a string of headlights stabbing the evening shadows.

Chelsea looked up at the moon and said wistfully, 'I wish this could last forever. It's like a fairy tale.'

Diamond agreed, but kept to himself the thought that it wouldn't last long unless he could take out Leon Greco.

Ashore, one pair of headlights kept

pace with the stern-wheeler. Beau Haggar was smiling all over his whiskered face because he had just recognized Diamond leaning over the deck rail.

15

Bank Score

The clock on the wall of the escort service lounge appeared to have stopped. Leon Greco stared hard at the sweep of the red seconds hand; it hadn't. Waiting for Madden to call back with news of his operation made time seem to crawl.

He was tensed up, lit a Cuban cigar and tried to relax in the large comfortable armchair. It should have been easy to relax because the air-conditioned lounge was filled with attractive and expensive young ladies, also waiting for the telephone to ring.

It was evening and the lighting was as discreet as the escort service. Each girl was well-groomed, smartly dressed and assumed a friendly smile; they might have been secretaries to senior executives. Each had a small overnight bag beside her chair. Some smoked with that sophisticated air of the professional model, some glanced through fashion magazines, others watched TV with the sound turned down. They didn't go in much for chatting among themselves.

The telephone rang and heads looked up. The manager, a blond bearded young man in a tuxedo answered smoothly:

'Pussy Cat Escort Agency . . . yes sir, Beverley is available . . . your address sir?' She scribbled on a pad, tore off the sheet and held it up. 'Certainly sir . . . about half-an-hour.'

A tall redhead in a lime green suit picked up her overnight bag, collected the address slip and went out swing, through the swing door.

Greco thought of Kenny waiting in the Ford outside; he'd eye the redhead as she passed and indulge in another of his fantasies. And run a mile if a flesh-and-blood woman tried to get him into bed.

Grecco smoked his cigar and waited for news, good news he hoped — and why shouldn't it be? The team he'd put together was first class and Madden was an experienced organiser. So assume it went well and he collected ten percent of — what? Madden wouldn't cheat; he had his reputation to consider and it would be reported in the papers. Big money anyway.

He looked at the clock again, wondering how much he would get. Ash fell onto his new suit, charcoal-grey with the faintest hint of red stripe, and he brushed it off.

The telephone rang again.

'Pussy Cat Escort Agency . . . yes sir, a credit card is acceptable . . . yes sir, we do have a black-skinned girl . . . I'm sure Coral will give every satisfaction . . . the Hilton . . . in half-an-hour sir, and thank you.'

A voluptuous negress wearing a dark blue evening dress picked up her bag, collected the slip and swept out of the lounge.

Greco watched the wall clock and sweated. All right, assume this first operation was a success, then he could expect more business to follow. He dreamed a little, his own home and office — a fixed address with no risk attached

— and one organiser after another asking him to put a team together.

He couldn't wait to get out of the rackets — even this escort agency. Since Diamond had hit on him, things were falling apart, too many of his managers trying to set up on their own. And he wasn't getting any younger. Now the cops were snooping around, sticking their noses into his business.

Well, Diamond was as good as taken care of. Haggar wasn't the sort to give up. He was a real black-hater, and he'd keep after Diamond till he nailed him.

The telephone rang.

'Pussy Cat Escort Agency . . . ' The blond young man held out the receiver.

Greco took it and heard Madden's voice. He stopped sweating and put down his cigar. Now he could relax.

★   ★   ★

The First National Bank in Baton Rouge was on North Boulevard, not far from the junction with Nicholson. This Friday morning the sun shone and traffic was light, pedestrians few — most people were already at work. It was just after opening time when a Pontiac drew up and parked outside the main door.

A young and obviously pregnant woman got out of the back; she looked as if she'd dressed in a hurry and the hands holding a small drugstore package were agitated. A clean-shaven man in an executive-style suit and carrying a brief-case followed her into the bank. The driver remained at the wheel with the engine running.

The uniformed security man standing just inside the doorway looked up sharply, then smiled and said, 'Good morning, Mrs. Taverner.'

She didn't answer, but hurried to the manager's office and entered without knocking. The man with the briefcase followed her inside and closed the door.

The manager stared in surprise. 'Claire — ?'

He half-rose in his swivel chair as Claire Taverner said, 'I've brought them,' and held out the package.

The manager looked bewildered, 'What — ?'

Madden made one quick movement, covering his face with a stocking mask. So far she had been too upset to look closely at him, but the situation was about to change. A second swift movement opened his briefcase and he brought out a sawn-off shotgun.

'This is a hold-up,' he said clearly and pointed the gun at Claire's bulging stomach.

The bank manager gaped in disbelief; his daughter's face turned ashen.

Madden's cold grey eyes watched them over the twin barrels.

'You a hunter, Mr. Fisher?' The manager nodded. 'Then I don't have to tell you what a double load of twelve-gauge Double-O buckshot will do to your daughter's womb. You'll lose both your only daughter and your unborn grand-child. If you remain calm and do exactly as I say, she won't be hurt — try for an alarm or waste time and I'll pull both triggers. Maybe you'd better take one of those pills now.'

Claire said dully, 'He told me you'd had another heart attack and needed your pills in a hurry.'

Fisher made a tight smile. 'I'm all right, Claire — relax if you can. I shan't do anything to put you at risk.'

Madden said: 'You've got the bills ready for people cashing their pay cheques? Is the vault open yet?'

'Yes, and yes.'

'Right then, this is what you'll do. You'll organise your tellers to work for me — they'll put the notes into plastic bags. By now, I'll have three men in the bank and they'll provide the bags. Don't bother with the small stuff — just twenties and up, the lot, understand?'

Fisher nodded, and sighed. 'I understand, and I'll do exactly as you say.'

'That's fine. If nobody tries any clever stuff, no one gets hurt. You're on your own — you tell your people what to do and make damn sure they do it right and fast. Just remember I'll be with your only daughter and that I'll blast her belly wide open at the first false move. Ready?'

Fisher moistened his lips. 'I'm ready.

Try not to worry, Claire, nothing will happen to you.'

He stood up behind his desk, crossed to the door and opened it. He stepped through, into the public section of the bank and raised his voice so that everyone would hear.

'May I have your attention, please?'

Business was temporarily suspended as all eyes turned to him. He was acutely aware of Claire behind him and the shotgun behind her.

He moistened his lips again. 'Please, please don't anyone make a wrong move. This man has a shotgun on my daughter!'

Two men stopped pretending to fill in forms, opened briefcases and whipped on stocking masks. They pulled out large black plastic bags and stepped up to the counter.

A third masked man moved up to the security guard and removed his revolver from its holster. 'Just to avoid temptation, pal,' he murmured. With gloved hands, he pinned a notice to the street door:

BANK CLOSED
Due to an electronic fault
We regret the inconvenience
Open at Noon

As he closed the door, he caught a glimpse of the waiting Pontiac. Ted Paley was revving his engine and both doors facing the sidewalk were open.

The robbery went smoothly. At Fisher's instruction, the tellers stuffed bundles of banknotes into the plastic bags; there were six bags, extra strong with a quick-release fastening at the neck.

Madden stood alone, shotgun placed against the lower part of Claire's back; she was pale and sweating. He watched the customers; an elderly man in a hard-worn suit, a burly guy in overalls, a couple of teenagers. They waited like statues. He looked at the hands of the wall-clock, calculating.

'Enough,' he said.

The three masked men took two bags each, secured the tops and carried them, one in each hand to the main door.

'You will all face away from the door,' Madden said.

The robbers waited till he was obeyed, then whipped off their masks and hurried outside.

Madden walked Claire Tavernier towards the front door, and paused.

'No heroics, please. If no one panics, nobody gets hurt. We're leaving now — and I suggest you don't poke a head outside for at least three minutes.'

He glanced past the half-open doorway; his men were already in the car with the bags. He whipped off his mask.

'Sorry to scare you, lady,' he murmured, and ran down the steps.

The get-away car was moving before he had the door shut. Paley, cool as a Grand Prix driver, rapidly built up speed, turned at the intersection and accelerated out of town.

In the back of the Pontiac, Hendriks, Woody and Violets were busy transferring banknotes into briefcases.

Madden watched the rearview mirror. 'No one yet.'

'They won't be long,' Paley said, his foot hard down.

The car kept going till the Louisiana State University showed ahead, then Madden cautioned: 'All right, take it easy now. We've got the time.'

Paley slowed to cruising speed and turned into the huge University lot where upwards of a hundred cars were parked in neat rows. He pulled up alongside a Buick with Skip waiting at the wheel.

They changed cars in seconds. Then sitting sedately with briefcases on their laps, they headed back towards Baton Rouge. The Buick cruised at a moderate speed as police cars, sirens screaming, rocketed by in the opposite direction. Skip drove down to the levee and parked out of the sun while they waited for the steamboat.

*　*　*

Detective Cave sat in his Plymouth, chewing an indigestion tablet and reading the *Times-Picayune*. His stomach was acting up again. Why was it he couldn't be bothered to eat a decent meal? Always hamburgers or the Colonel's fried chicken or some damn pizza.

From where he sat he had a view of Pierre's, on Decatur. Greco had the resources to put the boot in, and Cave wondered why he hadn't. Turk had gone to ground and Diamond was out of town and nothing much seemed to be happening. His pale eyes flicked from the restaurant front to his paper and the lead story.

DARING DAYLIGHT RAID

Mr. T. Fisher, manager of the First National Bank and his daughter, Mrs. Claire Taverner, were the dupes of —

The car door opened and Breeze slid into the back seat.

'Reading about the Baton Rouge job, huh? Half a million in notes — Geez, some haul!'

Cave said sourly, 'It's not my worry, thank God. We've got enough crime here, without borrowing from the capital.'

'Yeah?' The informer's voice held a note of slyness. 'A real pro job, smooth with no leads to follow. They got clear away — so who got it all together then?'

'An organiser, of course. Could be any one of a dozen.'

Breeze pushed back long floppy hair from his eyes. 'Maybe there's a new one in town,' he said softly. 'I hear a lot of rumours on my rounds — and one says Greco was spotted talking to a couple of bank job specialists just recently. It's only a rumour, mind.'

He slid from the car and merged with a bunch of tourists as though he were one of them.

Cave set his Plymouth in motion, turned up Esplanade to Rampart Street and drove past the Louis Armstrong Paris. He cruised automatically, his eyes registering the scene but his mind fitting together pieces of the jigsaw.

If Breeze's rumour had any truth, it looked like Greco was branching out — and that would account for his half-hearted attempts to keep his managers in line. And sometime, someone else would make a bid to take over. Right now would be a good time to put on the pressure.

Was Greco setting up as an organiser? Not likely. An employment agency?

Fred Cave thought that idea had the ring of truth as he followed the traffic flow. It excited him. There might be something for him there, a way to set up Greco so Diamond could reach him.

Meanwhile, a clean-up was scheduled. He broke away from the traffic, smiling, and headed for Police Headquarters; he wanted to put his idea to Lieutenant Stoner.

16

Live Bait

The moon hung above the Mississippi like a yellow globe in the summer darkness. The *Queen of the South* lay hard against a stone jetty, moored for the night; there was a gangway lowered to allow passengers who had the inclination to stroll along the river bank.

It was quiet except for the lapping of water against the jetty and a background murmur of conversation. The band had packed in for the night and most of the tourists had gone to their cabins. Mosquitoes whined about the gleam of swamps and, on the shore road, cars passed with a dazzle of headlights. A few couples huddled together in shadowed corners.

Chelsea Hull leaned on the deck rail and stared into the night; the moon's reflection rippled in dark water and bright stars pierced the sky. Behind her, twin funnels reared, tall and slender and rimmed with brass. It was the first time she'd played upriver and she was pleasantly relaxed and humming Vince's final number, happy to be waiting for Wash to join her. Their jazz had been good.

She couldn't remember feeling so content with life. Just to be out of the city, with no pressures, watching the shifting surface of the great river as it raced south to the Mexican Gulf. She promised herself she would sing with a riverboat band as often as she could get a date. It was a great life.

No Vogel, no Leon Greco, no Detective Cave; she had Wash to herself for a while . . . he seemed to be taking the investigation bit seriously, checking on those convention types who came aboard at Baton Rouge.

She glanced idly at the jetty where a station wagon was parked without lights. There was a shadow inside and she smiled, imagining a pair of lovers.

Cloud passed across the moon and she

heard a car door squeak, then footsteps on the gangway. A man's footsteps. She smelt whisky and the sourness of dirty clothes and an unwashed body.

A hand touched her arm and a voice with a Southern whine asked, 'Chelsea?'

She peered into the dark but could not make out much. 'Yes.'

Then the moon came out and she wished she were not alone on deck. She saw a stubbled face and looked into lecherous eyes. She tried to break away, but the claw-like hand was stronger than it looked.

'Let me go!'

She brought up her knee, but his body was turned so she only connected with his thigh.

'I've handled gals like you before,' the man said, and leered.

She turned her head, looking for help, and saw Diamond come up the steps from the lower deck.

'Wash!'

Diamond started, then moved forward.

Chelsea felt herself lifted and hugged tightly as the Southerner ran down the gangway and across the jetty to the station wagon. It didn't help that she was small; she felt like a doll, the way he slung her in the passenger seat and drove off.

She twisted around and saw Diamond running after the car. She tried the far door — locked — and then made a grab for the handbrake. The driver slammed his elbow into her solar plexus, knocking the breath out of her and doubling her up in pain.

'Wash'll kill you, Whitey,' she gasped, eyes watering.

'He'll try,' the redneck admitted, watching his rearview mirror.

Diamond was falling behind. The station wagon slowed and Diamond gained ground in great loping strides. Then it turned off the road onto a bumpy dirt track between overhanging branches. There was deep shadow with only faint streaks of moonlight filtering through a dense canopy of leaves. Chelsea could smell a bayou as she bounced about.

It was a totally deserted area, silent except for a buzz of insects. The car stopped and the driver gripped her arm and dragged her out, holding her with one hand and carrying a rifle in the other. Rifle . . . this had to be the man who'd shot Wash.

There was a footpath, partially overgrown, leading between live oaks. He pushed her along in front of him as he moved into cover. Chelsea tried to call a warning but her lungs wheezed and only a murmur came out.

'Shout all you want, gal,' her captor encouraged.

She pressed her lips together and prayed; now she knew she was bait in a trap . . .

Diamond's chest heaved and sweat trickled under his shirt. He rested a moment beside the empty station wagon, getting his breath back and allowing time for his eyes to adjust to the gloom under the trees. There was no hurry now that the man who had grabbed Chelsea was on foot; it was a time for caution.

He exercised his left arm gently; the wound was healing nicely but he hoped he wouldn't have to use it.

The moon made a faint shimmer of

light on broad leaves and there was a sound of trickling water nearby. He reminded himself the bayou was part swampland, that he couldn't afford to go blundering about in the dark. He peered along the footpath; shadows shifted, making a confused pattern of light and shade.

He started to think for the first time since he'd chased after Chelsea and the man who had grabbed her. Maybe, just maybe there was more to it than the rape of a black gal by one of the Klan. Could be she was a decoy. He remembered the Southern voice on the telephone that had lured him to a parking lot on Front Street. The rifleman . . . and the hairs on the back of his neck bristled.

Diamond decided to play it sneaky. He moved off silently, recalling his training in Vietnam; avoiding patches of moonlight and gently bending back projecting branches; watching where he put his feet, avoiding fallen twigs and pools of water. He glided through the dark like a shadow, sure as a hunting cat. And now he was glad of his black skin.

He wanted to get his hands on the Southerner before he hurt Chelsea — but he had to stay alive to help her. And his sixth sense warned him it was a trap he was moving into. There was almost certainly a rifle muzzle waiting for him at the end of the trail.

He pulled his revolver free of its holster as he eased his way forward.

The path petered out in a clearing, moonlit, with the dark trunks of trees rising like a wall around it. He heard a movement somewhere ahead, and froze. The stench of the bayou was getting to be overpowering.

Vines dangled from high branches. A frog croaked. Then a bullet winged past his head and tore the leaves.

A voice swore, then jeered: 'Ah'm gonna screw your gal real good.'

Diamond crouched like a track runner ready to sprint.

'Ah know's you're out there, Diamond, and I've got a rifle at her back . . . see?'

Diamond peered between dripping leaves. Moonlight gleamed on Chelsea's coffee-brown face as she was pushed forward; she looked mad enough to spit. The unknown man was behind her, using her body as a shield.

'Jest drop your gun, Diamond, and step out where I can see yuh — and do it now or she gets a slug in the spine!'

Diamond shifted his position quietly. The man didn't know exactly where he was, so he still had a chance. He straightened up, measuring the distance he had to travel, then tossed his revolver to one side of the clearing. The rifleman's eyes tracked it automatically — and Diamond came hurtling from the undergrowth in a savage spring.

Chelsea slammed the rifle barrel sideways as it was triggered, wrenched herself free and dropped flat.

Diamond went over her and hit the man like an enraged elephant. They both sprawled in the mud and wet leaves and Diamond grabbed the rifle and tore it out of the Southerner's hands.

'Chelsea?'

'Goddamn it, my hair's ruined!'

The would-be assassin rolled into shadow, swearing under his breath, then he was up and running. Diamond swung the rifle barrel around and loosed off a shot. Cloud covered the moon and, in the darkness, Diamond said, 'Stay put, baby, I'll be back for you,' and went hunting.

Somewhere ahead, he heard his quarry crashing through a tangle of under-growth. With no rifle and no hostage, the hunter became the hunted, and it sounded as though he weren't enjoying the change.

Diamond smiled grimly as he pressed on with his silent pursuit; if Chelsea was worrying about her hair she wasn't seriously hurt. He heard the slosh of legs through water, a rasping of breath, and knew he was closing the gap. It seemed as if the Southerner was in a panic.

Diamond lifted the rifle muzzle and fired another shot, just to let him know he was right behind. The thrashing noises became desperate; then there followed a silence, as if the hunted man was no longer sure of his way.

Diamond crept through marsh grass and reeds in the dark. He smelt brackish water and Spanish moss hung like an eerie mist in the occasional shaft of moonlight. From close at hand came an unpleasant sucking sound and a bout of violent cursing.

Diamond took a step forward . . . and stepped back hurriedly as mud sucked viciously at his shoes.

The would-be assassin was not so lucky. He'd moved too far into the swamp and was trapped, sinking slowly deeper as he struggled to free himself. The more agitated his movements, the deeper he sank into a slimy ooze.

Diamond leaned against a tree and watched. The man was already up to his waist in stinking mud when he managed to reach a trailing vine, gripped it desperately and tried to pull himself up. The vine broke like a frayed cord and he gave a sobbing gasp as he settled deeper into the swamp.

The thick dark semi-liquid was up to his armpits and he held his arms out, hoping for a last minute rescue.

He saw Diamond waiting, and called, 'Help me . . . please.'

Diamond smiled bleakly. 'You want to

tell me who paid you?'

'It was Greco . . . Leon Greco . . . help . . . '

The mud reached his chin and his last word turned into a scream that cut off as he swallowed and choked. His eyes bulged, pleading for his life, pleading with one of the race he hated.

Death was a great leveler, Diamond mused; it treated black and white alike.

He watched the eyes submerge, then the top of the head. He chucked the rifle into the swamp and began to retrace his steps. There was still Greco to settle with.

It began to rain before he reached Chelsea.

17

Set-up

Cave walked into the detective's squad-room, tipped back his Panama with a carefree gesture and lit a Marlboro. One of the officers working at a VDU looked up and said, 'Hi, Fred. How's tricks?'

'Fine, just fine,' Cave returned, walked along the aisle between desks and tapped lightly at Stoner's door.

'Come in.'

Cave opened the door and went in, almost jauntily, and perched on one corner of the lieutenant's desk.

Stoner leaned back and regarded him through rimless spectacles and asked, with deceptive mildness: 'Yes, Fred, what is it?'

'I've just heard an interesting story. It looks like Greco might be behind the Baton Rouge job. If so, that explains a lot of things. And now would be a good time to really put some pressure on the rackets — if my informant is right, there's a chance that at least some of them will fall apart.'

Stoner sipped coffee from a plastic cup. 'What are you trying to promote now?' he asked coldly. 'And where's that enforcer of yours got to?'

'Private investigator,' Cave corrected. 'He's out of town right now.'

'So he runs when the going gets tough?'

'You've seen him, lieutenant. D'you want to repeat that to his face? He got shot and had his office fire-bombed, remember?'

'And you thought we could tie the gun that killed Earl Vogel to Kenny. You thought wrong. Fred. You've got Greco on the brain. He's only one man — he can't be responsible for every crime in this city.'

'No, just most of the organised crime.' Cave's face twisted in a sour grimace. 'But you don't want to know. Has he got you in his pocket or something?'

'I'll forget you said that, Fred. This

time. You know goddamn well Greco's got a high-powered lawyer — and he's too smart to get personally involved. I need evidence that'll stand up in court. You bring me proof and I'll act fast enough to please even you. Now get the hell off my desk and out of here.'

Cave's face wrinkled in a scowl and, puffing on his cigarette he slid upright and stalked from the office.

Lieutenant Harry Stoner contemplated his desk blotter for some moments, then drained his coffee. Cave had a thing about Greco, sure, but he was right; Leon Greco was behind most of the organised crime in New Orleans and it seemed the law just couldn't touch him.

Maybe Cave's informant was right, maybe there was a chance this time. A little pressure here and they might just get things jumping.

He reached for the telephone.

★   ★   ★

Diamond's foot tapped rhythmically to a Fats Waller number on the record player;

225

even Fats singing and playing *Pan-Pan* couldn't quite get his mind off his itching arm. But that, he told himself, was a good sign; the wound was healing.

Dressed casually in T-shirt and cotton slacks, he sat opposite Chelsea, sipping coffee while she brushed her hair. Beyond the window the rain was still coming down.

After getting out of the swamp he'd driven the station wagon back to the city, holed up in her apartment on Esplanade and phoned Cave a brief outline of what had happened. Then they'd made love, showered and eaten a large steak apiece, celebrating their getting back alive.

His revolver cleaned and reloaded, they waited behind a locked door for the detective to arrive. The room looked even more chaotic than usual, littered with mudstained clothes and dirty plates.

Diamond wanted only one thing now that Chelsea had been put in danger; a showdown with Leon Greco.

'You'll have to collect your trumpet from Vince,' Chelsea said.

'Yeah.' It wasn't the first thing Diamond had on his mind. 'Later.'

The doorbell rang. He turned down the volume on the record player and picked up his revolver. 'Who is it?'

'Cave.'

Diamond opened the door on the chain, checking before he unfastened the chain to let the detective in. He relocked the door.

Cave beat water from his Panama and hung his raincoat on the hallstand. Silently, Chelsea brought him a can of cold beer, determined not to like this wrinkled little cop who had got her man into so much trouble.

'Thanks.' Cave took a seat. 'Sure is a misery out right now.' He pulled the tab, and took a long swallow and got down to business. 'I checked out the station wagon. It belongs to an old-fashioned Southern hunter by the name of Haggar — a real black hater.'

'Well, he won't hunt or hate again,' Diamond said flatly. 'He went into the swamp over his head. And that leaves Greco.'

Cave made a thin smile. 'Greco's got other things on his mind at the moment — the lieutenant's moving against his rackets. Now give me the full story, every detail.'

He listened with a thoughtful expression and when Diamond's exposition ended, murmured, 'Well, I reckon nobody's ever going to find Haggar's body.' An idea stirred and he thought: there's more than one way to skin a rabbit. 'Yeah, it could work out.'

He drained his beer and switched his attention back to Diamond.

'Now listen, this is what you'll do. Tomorrow, you ask around at two-three places you know for the Fox. With the department already clamping down, that'll throw him even more off balance. Keep on the move and don't go near him until I set it up. Reckon I'll be able to hand him to you on a plate.'

'Make it soon,' Diamond said. 'I shan't feel Chelsea's safe till this is finished.'

Cave rose and went for his hat and coat. 'Sooner than you think,' he said briskly. 'One more thing — when you get

Greco alone, make him talk. If he was involved in the Baton Rouge heist — '

Diamond gave an exclamation. 'I forgot! I was too worried about Chelsea . . . six men came aboard at Baton Rouge, carrying briefcases. They didn't look to me like businessmen attending a convention.'

Cave paused at the door as Chelsea turned up the volume and Fats on piano.

'Yeah, well, the bank's offering a reward for the recovery of their money. What you'll need are names to go with the faces. You might do yourself a bit of good, talking to Mr. Greco.'

★ ★ ★

Next morning, Diamond used a taxi to collect his car and then delivered Chelsea to the *Black Swan* for a rehearsal. After collecting his trumpet from Vince Norman, he set out to tour the city. Rain came down steadily and the sidewalks were almost deserted.

The Mustang's wipers gave him a blurred image of steak-bars and theatres, gaudy neons advertising funeral parlours and McDonalds.

He stopped first at Nick's Arcade and ducked through the rain into the clatter of slot machines and gamblers with lost expressions, oblivious to him and the weather.

Only the moneychanger and Nick were in the back office and Nick, his arm in a plaster cast, eyed him warily.

'I heard you'd quit, Wash.'

'You heard right so relax, man. You've nothing to fear from me.'

'Yeah?' Nick smiled nervously and looked at the telephone on his desk. 'That right you're with the cops now?'

Diamond shook his head. 'Strictly private, and it's information I want. D'you have any idea where I can catch up with Leon?'

'He keeps on the move — you know that. I wouldn't know where to find him right now.'

'Guess I'll ask somewhere else then.'

'Yeah, you do that, Wash.'

Diamond walked past slot machines and out to his car, smiling; he guessed the arcade manager would be on the phone right away.

He drove through drenching rain, past a go-go bar, a blue movie house and a drugstore, to Irene's massage parlour and walked inside.

Irene was at the desk, watching TV; she looked at him and pursed her lips in a lemon-sour expression and said: 'You're not welcome here, Wash. Christ, even with your thick skin you must have caught on that you're not the boss's number one favourite.'

Diamond shrugged. 'Too bad.'

From the cubicles off the passage leading back a couple of young girls in bikini briefs looked out, assessing him as a potential customer.

'I'm not starving for a bit of loving,' he said. 'And I don't reckon to pay for it anyway.'

'I hear you're some kind of cop now.' Irene patted her platinum hair and sniffed. 'Don't think you're going to shake me down for any pay-off.'

'I'm only after information. I just called in to see if you can locate Greco for me.'

Irene smoothed down her tight black dress and smiled. 'He'd thank me for that? Nothing doing, Wash — just beat it, huh?'

'Why sure, Irene, sure.'

Diamond walked outside, grinning hugely. Leon Greco was about to get another phone call any minute. And he'd start worrying, wondering what was going on. At least he'd know now that his hitman had failed.

Diamond drove across town in pouring rain, to the suburbs. Metairie was mostly a residential area and there were still some fine old houses left. Beyond a row of picturesque trees, he parked outside Oscar's Gymnasium. Inside was a smell of old leather and stale sweat.

'Hi, Wash,' Oscar greeted him. 'You ain't been in for a workout lately.'

'I've been busy. Turk around?'

Oscar stroked his bald head. 'Hell no, he sorta left town in a hurry. I thought you'd have heard.'

'A little bird whispered it might be so.' Diamond admitted. 'You know where I can get hold of Greco?'

Oscar looked startled. 'Who can tell where that man is? Riding around in his car, like always, I suppose.'

'Yeah, well, I might as well work out a bit while I'm here.'

'You're welcome.'

Diamond stripped and changed, used the punchbag and the cycle machine till he got a sweat on. He noticed Oscar disappear into his office, and guessed he was on the phone to Greco. He indulged in a hot and cold shower and felt good; his injured arm was now no more than a dull ache. Enough to remind him he still had to be careful.

He was willing to bet he felt a lot better than Leon Greco right now, and hummed *Tiger Rag* as he dressed and went out to his Mustang.

★   ★   ★

Leon Greco was not feeling happy. He sat behind a desk in an upstairs room of a gambling club, alternately watching the rain come down beyond the window and a view of the tables on closed-circuit TV.

His stomach felt uneasy and he crushed out a half-smoked cigar, and put an anti-acid tablet in his mouth; he didn't think he could take a lot more stress.

The cops were putting more pressure on for some reason. And now, apparently, Haggar had failed and Diamond was back in town and asking around for him. Surely he didn't believe he could get close to him? He wished he knew what had happened with Beau Haggar . . .

As if he didn't have enough problems with his managers.

And no enforcer. He was definitely unhappy with the situation.

Behind him, Kenny stopped studying the centrefold of his new girlie magazine and said viciously, 'It was a mistake hiring that Southerner, Mr. Greco. You should have given the job to me — say the word and I can still take out that black.'

The lanky bodyguard snatched his revolver from a shoulder holster. 'What about it?'

He sounded too eager and Greco was about to remind him that Diamond had taken a gun away from him once before, when the telephone rang. He scooped it up and said, non-committally, 'Yes?'

He didn't recognise the voice at the other end. 'A mutual acquaintance passed me this number — fellar you did a job for concerning the capital.'

Capital . . . Baton Rouge . . . it had to be another organiser. Leon Greco felt better immediately. Madden must have passed the word.

'It's nice to hear from you, Mr. — ?'

'Abbott, you call me Abbott. It's like this — I'm connected with security and I need to get a team together. D'you think you can provide the right men for that sort of job?'

'I'm sure I can, Mr. Abbott,' Greco said smoothly. 'I can put a team together for you. It's no problem.'

'That's fine. Maybe we should meet to discuss details?'

'I'm agreeable,' the Fox said. 'It'll be out of town, I assume?'

'Surely. And I've picked a good spot, somewhere we won't be disturbed. This is how you get to it . . . '

18

Killing Ground

The Ford's windshield wipers flicked from side to side with the hypnotic effect of a metronome. The monotonous beat almost lulled Leon Greco to sleep as he relaxed in the back of the car. He unwrapped a fresh Cuban cigar and ran it under his nose, savouring the aroma before lighting it. Water trickled down the windows, forming endlessly changing patterns and blurring the view of the country outside.

At the wheel, Kenny stared forward in concentration; the road was awash with water as the rain bucketed down. From time to time, as he gained a clear view ahead, he muttered to himself, completely immersed in his sexual fantasies.

Greco felt better now he was out of the city. It was great to get the chance of another job so quickly; Madden must really have been impressed to pass the word along so fast. Set this new job up, he thought, and he'd definitely break away from all the rackets. The cops were bearing down like they scented blood.

He allowed himself a brief fantasy. First thing, he'd get out of New Orleans and set up a base someplace else . . . Kansas City maybe. He could operate an employment agency from anywhere. Get himself a fine house, a regular woman; providing organisers with a team was risk-free.

The road followed the Mississippi inland and there were few cars out in the downpour. The river was running fast, not far below the top of the bank; a few more inches and it would spill over onto the highway. The car's tyres hissed through a layer of water.

'Take it easy, Kenny,' he said, glancing at his watch. 'We're ahead of time and I want to get there in one piece.'

He wasn't keen on Kenny driving him to the meeting place, but there wasn't much choice. It was years since he'd driven a car and he wasn't risking his neck learning again on a wet road in this weather. Neither did he want a cab driver to know where he was going. He'd have to pay Kenny off shortly anyway.

The Ford slowed and began to creep along. Greco peered through wet glass; God, but Abbott had picked a lonely spot. The tyres sent up a shower of spray as Kenny pulled over to the side and stopped.

'This looks like the place, Mr. Greco.'

The Fox stared at an overnight mooring for steamboats. There the river took a winding course. Set back from the road was an old house, isolated from the water by dense undergrowth; it might have been a planter's home long ago but now looked derelict.

'Stay in the car, Kenny.'

His driver immediately picked up a new magazine and turned the pages, staring bug-eyed.

Greco opened the door and the wet heat slapped him in the face. He scurried towards the broken down veranda, fat drops of warm rain pelting him, his cigar spluttering. The dank smell of a bayou wafted from the direction of a wall of tangled vegetation. He looked up as he reached the bottom of a short flight of wooden steps. He heard the creak of unoiled hinges as a door opened and when he saw who waited for him, he threw down his cigar and shouted:

'Kenny! It's . . . '

Washington T. Diamond stood in the doorway at the top of the rickety steps, smiling coldly over the barrel of a levelled revolver. Cave's deception as the organiser, Abbott, had worked to perfection; he had the Fox right where he wanted him.

The lanky bodyguard came fast out of the Ford, drawing his gun as he ran through the rain. He fired as he came, screaming, 'I'll get you, Diamond! I'll — '

Diamond ignored the lead slamming into the woodwork around him; not even Kenny could aim straight on the run. He stood motionless, holding his revolver rock steady with both arms full out before him, took careful aim and squeezed off a single shot.

Kenny went down with an extra bloody eye in his forehead.

Leon Greco moaned and began to run, around the side of the house and into the cover of the undergrowth. His dream had foundered and he was scared. Always before there had been a body between him and any threat to his life — and now Kenny had failed him. As he ran, he smelt of fear.

Diamond let him go, confident he couldn't get far. He dragged Kenny's body under cover and moved the Ford out of sight; he didn't want any curious passerby sticking his nose in. Then he followed Greco into the bayou.

The Fox was easy to follow. He'd panicked and his blundering path was as clear as a swathe scythed through the brush. Diamond took it easy, knowing he'd catch up before long, giving him all the time in the world to imagine death reaching for him. He wanted Greco reduced to a blob of shivering jelly.

Diamond hummed *Twelfth Street Rag* as he ghosted between trees hung with Spanish moss like a gauze veil. He was glad he'd stopped along the way for a large bowl of gumbo, chicken soup thickened with okra. He pushed through broad palm leaves and bushes, gun in hand. A vile stink arose from brackish water as if something had died and rotted there. Small rodent eyes watched him pass.

The ground was marshy and he trod warily, remembering what had happened to Beau Haggar. Rain dripped from branches that became a waterfall in every clearing.

As he squelched through soft sticky mud he glimpsed an alligator, grey snout breaking the surface of the bayou.

It was hot and humid and his shirt stuck to him. The dark canopy made visibility poor and, the further he penetrated the everglades, the more Diamond was reminded of the green hell of Vietnam. He was soaked to the skin and sweat poured off him.

He pushed on, past mangroves with swollen roots with insects buzzing about his ears. He heard a distant screech of wildfowl. Beyond a clump of canes he caught sight of Greco, barely ahead of him. The Fox was out of condition for this kind of slog, winded and gasping for breath, his expensive thin-soled shoes slipping and sliding in the mud. Diamond closed the gap between them like a remorseless Nemesis.

Vines straggled along cypress and oak as he ploughed through a rank-smelling sludge of rotting vegetation. Greco paused, leaning on the bole of a tree, looking wildly about. His pale face glistened with moisture and his eyes showed terror as he watched Diamond loom out of the rain-curtain, revolver cocked and ready.

His legs trembled and he staggered as he lurched into motion, trying to get away. He had a stitch in his side, but he kept going, driven by fear. His legs buckled and he grasped at a sapling, panting for breath. Knowing he couldn't escape, he turned in desperation, pleading.

'Five thousand bucks, Wash . . . ten thousand . . . I'll pay you anything you ask, anything . . . just let me live.'

Diamond lifted his revolver and took careful aim. His finger tightened on the trigger. Greco had put Chelsea at risk and didn't deserve to live. Then he remembered Cave's words — 'What you'll need are names to go with the faces' — and paused.

'Names,' he said flatly. 'Give me the names of the men involved in the bank robbery in Baton Rouge.'

The Fox stared at him with disbelief showing in his eyes. How could Diamond — how could anyone — know that he'd got Madden's team together? He'd been so careful . . .

Diamond took a step closer and the barrel of his revolver loomed huge and threatening.

Greco babbled, reeling off names. 'Madden was the organiser. Blackie Hendriks, Ted Paley, Woody, Skip and Violets.'

Diamond smiled in the rain, on his way to the reward money, and it was like a shark showing a mouthful of teeth; he felt good seeing Greco reduced from untouchable to nothing. He remembered Pierre's blind daughter, his cats slashed and gutted, his office burned down and

Chelsea used as bait to trap him.

And put his revolver back in its holster.

Greco sighed with relief, swaying. 'That's good, Wash, good. I'll see you right — '

Diamond laid big black hands on him and lifted him bodily into the air.

'Wash! What are you . . . doing?'

With contemptuous ease, Diamond hurled him far out into the bayou. Greco landed with a splash, and sank. When he surfaced, he spat out muddy water.

'Help! I can't swim!'

He went under, bobbed up again.

A grey log-like form cut through the water with deceptive swiftness. A corrugated tail lashed the surface and great jaws opened to reveal ranks of shiny serrated teeth.

Leon Greco, fighting for air as he sank and rose again, saw the alligator coming for him. His eyes bulged and he screamed his terror. There was a flurry of white water, suddenly stained red as he was pulled down.

Diamond watched a hand rise briefly, as if waving goodbye, then that too vanished beneath the surface of the bayou.

We do hope that you have enjoyed reading this large print book.

Did you know that all of our titles are available for purchase?

We publish a wide range of high quality large print books including:
Romances, Mysteries, Classics General Fiction Non Fiction and Westerns

Special interest titles available in large print are:
The Little Oxford Dictionary Music Book, Song Book Hymn Book, Service Book

Also available from us courtesy of Oxford University Press:
Young Readers' Dictionary (large print edition) Young Readers' Thesaurus (large print edition)

For further information or a free brochure, please contact us at:
**Ulverscroft Large Print Books Ltd., The Green, Bradgate Road, Anstey, Leicester, LE7 7FU, England.
Tel:** (00 44) **0116 236 4325
Fax:** (00 44) **0116 234 0205**

DEATH OF A
LOW HANDICAP MAN

Brian Ball ✓

When Tom Tyzack is viciously beaten to death with a golf club on the local golf course, PC Arthur Root, the local village bobby, is in the unenviable position of having to question his fellow club members. He is regarded with scorn by the detective in charge of the case, and the latter's ill-natured attitude toward the suspects does little to assist him in solving the mystery. But it is Root who, after a second brutal murder, stumbles on the clue that leads to the discovery of the murderer's identity.

ONE SWORD LESS

Colin D. Peel

Working on a defence project in a Research Laboratory, electronic engineer Richard Brendon discovers that he has become part of the cold war. Agonisingly, Brendon is required to balance the lives of his wife and children against co-operation with a foreign power. Forced to use his technical expertise to further a plan to precipitate nuclear war, he takes desperate action to prevent the project and save millions of people from certain destruction.

POSTMAN'S KNOCK

J. F. Straker

Inspector Pitt has a problem. The postman in Grange Road has mysteriously vanished. Had he absconded with the mail — been kidnapped or perhaps murdered? And why had he delivered only some of the letters? The people of Grange Road seem averse to police inquiries. Was there a conspiracy to remove the postman? Before any questions are answered assault, blackmail and sudden death disturb the normal peace of Grange Road.

ONE TO JUMP

George Douglas

When Detective Sergeant Dick Garrett spends his leave in Wellesbourne Green to persuade ex-crook Molly Bilton to marry him, he is faced with a mystery. Ace criminal Flint, previously known to Molly, is found dead with no clues to the killer. An assault on Gypsy Ben Thompson's daughter leads Garrett to risk his future in the Force. He suspects that one of the local police could be involved working hand in glove with the dead man.

REFLECTED GLORY

John Russell Fearn

When artist Clive Hexley, R. A. vanishes, Chief Inspector Calthorp of Scotland Yard is called upon to look into the disappearance, and his investigations lead him to question Hexley's ex-fiancee, Elsa Farraday. Elsa confesses that she has murdered the artist. The girl's peculiar manner puzzles Calthorp, and he hesitates to make an arrest, particularly as Hexley's body cannot be found. It is not until Calthorp calls in Dr. Adam Castle, the psychiatrist investigator, that the strange mystery of Elsa's behaviour and the artist's disappearance is solved.